Joy Comes In The

Morning

Joy Comes In The Morning

Morning

Vanessa Miller

Book 2
Praise Him Anyhow Series

Other Books by Vanessa Miller

How Sweet The Sound
Heirs of Rebellion
The Best of All
Better for Us
Her Good Thing
Long Time Coming
A Promise of Forever Love
A Love for Tomorrow
Yesterday's Promise
Forgotten
Forgiven
Forsaken
Rain for Christmas (Novella)
Through the Storm
Rain Storm
Latter Rain
Abundant Rain
Former Rain

Anthologies (Editor)
Keeping the Faith
Have A Little Faith
This Far by Faith

EBOOKS
Love Isn't Enough

A Mighty Love

The Blessed One (Blessed and Highly Favored series)

The Wild One (Blessed and Highly Favored Series)

The Preacher's Choice (Blessed and Highly Favored Series)

The Politician's Wife (Blessed and Highly Favored Series)

The Playboy's Redemption (Blessed and Highly Favored Series)

Tears Fall at Night (Praise Him Anyhow Series)

Joy Comes in the Morning (Praise Him Anyhow Series)

A Forever Kind of Love (Praise Him Anyhow Series)

Ramsey's Praise (Praise Him Anyhow Series)

Escape to Love (Praise Him Anyhow Series)

Praise For Christmas (Praise Him Anyhow Series)

His Love Walk (Praise Him Anyhow Series)

1

Psalm 137: 1-4
By the rivers of Babylon, there we sat down, yea,
we wept, when we remembered Zion. We hanged our
harps upon the willows in the midst thereof.
For there they that carried us away captive
required of us a song; and they that wasted us required of
us mirth, saying, "Sing us one of the songs of Zion."
How shall we sing the Lord's song in a strange
land?

Joy Marshall strutted into the Municipal
Courthouse at 8:55 am, just minutes before the judge
would be seated. She was wearing the Michelle
Obama sleeveless dress look. And since she was a
P90X workout girl—with the t-shirt to prove it—Joy
had the arms to carry off such a look. Her hair was
pulled up on top of her head, giving her face an exotic
look that caused the law breakers and the law makers

in the courthouse to stop and stare. But Joy didn't even notice. She had one thing on her mind that morning… revenge. As far as Joy was concerned, revenge was best when served cold and she was about to serve up a heaping pile of it.

She hadn't spoken to her father in five years. He'd shown up at her law school graduation four years before, and Joy had turned her back to him when he tried to congratulate her. Her father had sent roses to her office when she had accepted an Assistant District Attorney position a year and a half ago, but Joy had sent the roses back. She'd also sent him a very unflattering picture of herself hugging a toilet and puking up her guts. She'd told her father that the picture represented the girl he had created… but he could never lay claim on the woman she would become.

Ramsey, her stepfather had taken that picture of Joy after one of her famous nights of drinking. The next morning he took her to breakfast at the same IHOP he'd taken her mother on their first, unofficial date. While Joy struggled to hold her head up, Ramsey slid the picture over to her. After taking a quick look at the picture, Joy's head started pounding. She ran her hands down her face, as a look of embarrassment crept up. "Where'd you get this?"

"I took it when you came home last night. I wanted you to see what a fine and upstanding woman you turned out to be."

She heard the sarcasm in his voice and didn't like it one bit. "Marrying my mother doesn't give you the right to get in my business. I'm a grown woman and prefer to be treated as one."

The waitress placed scrambled eggs and bacon in front of Ramsey and pancakes in front of Joy. When the waitress left their table, Ramsey said, "I'm not in the habit of treating people who live in my house like grown folk when they don't pay bills, and do nothing with their lives."

"I finished law school. Isn't that what my mother wanted? Okay, I did it, so stop harassing me."

Ramsey leaned back in his seat. He studied her for a moment and then let her have it, no holds barred. "Look Joy, I know that this adjustment has been hard on you... probably harder on you than anyone else, but you can't self-destruct over it."

What did he know about the pain she was dealing with? As far as Joy was concerned, her father hadn't just betrayed her mother when he cheated with Jasmine. He'd betrayed her as well, because she had looked up to her father and believed he could do no wrong. And then one day she discovered that he wasn't just doing wrong, but he was doing it with Joy's best friend. So in one crazy and heart-wrenching day, she'd lost not just her father and best friend... she'd lost her trust in mankind. And no matter how hard she tried, Joy just couldn't figure out how to get it back.

"Joy, I know that you're angry with your father, and you're trying to punish him for what he did to you. But you're going about this the wrong way."

Her stomach was not in the mood for food, so she pushed her plate away. But she was finally ready to listen to Ramsey. "What do you mean?"

"Success is the best revenge, Joy. Drinking yourself into an early grave is not going to hurt Nelson Marshall. You know what will stick in his gut, though? Show your father that you succeeded even though he chose to walk away."

Ramsey's words had so encouraged her, that Joy stopped drinking and put an honest effort towards finding a job. Now she was an Assistant District Attorney and today was the day that she would finally exact her revenge on her father.

The so-called Honorable Judge Nelson Marshall had been assigned to preside over her most recent case. When he saw her name, he should have recused himself on the spot, but since he chose not to do the right thing, as usual, Joy was about to do it for him.

"Good morning, Ms. Marshall. You're looking good today," a big bellied security guard, who obviously needed Ramsey to give him a good talking to so he could lay off the beers, said to her as she walked over to the security area.

"Thanks, Malcolm, how are you doing this morning?" Joy handed her Michael Kors handbag and briefcase to the security guard and prepared to go through the metal detectors.

"I'm doing good. Getting married next week," Malcolm told her as she walked through the metal detector.

Joy almost offered her condolences. But she reminded herself that not everyone viewed marriage as an apocalyptic occurrence. But they knew just as well as she did that over half of all marriages end in divorce. That includes the ones that claim to be Christian marriages, like the one her mother and father had, until the day he decided to leave her for his girlfriend. After her father had done his dirt and divorced her mother, Joy hadn't been able to look at marriage the same way. She'd even called off her own engagement to Troy Daniels and she'd been living happily single and not interested in mingling at all ever since. She didn't have time to go over all of her woes with Malcolm, so she simply said, "Congratulations. I wish you the best." Joy took her belongings and walked away from him as fast as she could.

Joy got on the elevator heading to the third floor. She walked into courtroom A, where Lance Bryant and his repeat offender were already seated and waiting on Judge Do-Wrong to make his royal appearance.

She caught Lance staring at her as she made her way to the prosecuting table. He was a fine brother with wavy hair and a beautiful smile, but she wasn't interested. Joy put her briefcase down as Lance leaned her way and said, "Long time no see... how've you been?"

Joy gave him a close lipped smile and then turned back to her paperwork. She had tried two other cases against Lance in the short time that she had been an Assistant DA. Lance seemed like a good guy, but he sure picked some loser clients. He handled everything from assault to robbery, and always seemed to believe that his clients were as innocent as new born babes.

"Oh, so it's like that, huh? You not speaking today? Guess you're still upset about that whuppin' you took the last time."

She'd won the first case, but Lance had, indeed, won the second case. Joy was actually thankful that Lance won that case, because as it turned out, his client had been falsely accused. But he wasn't about to win this case, not even close, nor was she about to deal with her father the entire week that it would take to wrap this case up.

"All rise," the bailiff said as Judge Nelson took his seat behind the bench.

Joy's fists instantly clenched as she watch her father sit in a chair he didn't deserve to be in. She had tried her best to get him out of that seat during the last two elections, but the people of North Carolina just kept voting the adulterer back in. A few years back, Joy had delighted in telling her father that she had been the one to provide the media with information about his girlfriend and his divorce. He'd tried to apologize to her for what he had done to their family, but she wasn't interested in hearing it.

Judge Nelson shuffled a few papers around as he avoided looking in Joy's direction. He then said, "All we are doing today is setting bail, so let's get to it."

Joy said, "I am not prepared to have a bail hearing yet."

Nelson took his glasses off and glanced in his daughter's direction. "What's the problem, Counselor?"

Joy smirked. Using the court in this manner could seriously damage her career, but she didn't care. Every chance she got, she was going to let her father know what an awful human being he was, and if anyone had a problem with it, she would simply start her own law firm. "You are the problem, Your Honor." As she said the words *Your Honor*, her eyes rolled and it was obvious to all present that she thought he was anything *but* honorable.

Nelson Marshall seemed to shrink in his seat for a moment. He closed his eyes and rubbed his temples. "This is not the time or place for this, Joy. You have a job to do and so do I. Let's just get on with it, all right?"

"No," Joy said flippantly. "You should have recused yourself from this case the moment you saw that I was the attorney of record, but since you didn't, I am now publicly asking that you recuse yourself."

"Am I missing something?" Lance asked as he looked from Judge Marshall to Joy. His client nudged him, and then whispered something in his ear.

"I see no reason why I should recuse myself. I am more than able to be an impartial judge in the matter that is before the court."

"It is well known that I informed the media about your marital misconduct, so if you do not recuse yourself, I will request a judicial review."

Lance lifted his hand in order to get the judge's attention. When Judge Marshall turned to him, Lance said, "If there is some sort of problem between you and the assistant DA, then I respectfully request that Attorney Joy Marshall recuse herself so that we can move forward with the case. My client is entitled to his day in court and he does not want to delay the process waiting for another judge to be assigned to the case."

Joy hadn't seen that coming. The defendant was entitled to a speedy trial, so his wishes might outweigh hers. She turned to Lance and said, "If the defendant is concerned about being able to post bond today, I am more than willing to work out bail with this judge."

Lance took her up on the offer. Bail was set for ten thousand and then Joy got back to her mission. "Now that we've handled that bit of business, I would like to reiterate the fact that I would like you to recuse yourself," she said to her father, the judge.

The defendant nudged Lance again. Lance spoke up again, "Your honor, if one of you has to go, my client would prefer that it be the prosecutor. He does not like the idea that his case would be delayed while he waits to be put on another judge's docket."

"What's his problem?" Joy asked indignantly. "If he makes bail, he'll be at home with his family and friends while he awaits a new trial date."

Lance turned back to Judge Marshall. "My client has a right to a speedy trial. His rights shouldn't be tossed aside at the whim of the prosecution."

Nelson turned to his daughter and said, "Well, Counselor?"

"Well what?" she snapped at her father, confused by the entire incident. Why on earth wouldn't a criminal be happy to have his court appearance moved back? He'd have more time to spend with his family and fellow criminal buddies before he is proven guilty and spends the next ten years behind bars.

"It looks like you're the one who needs to recuse," Nelson said to his daughter.

Joy threw up her hands, grabbed her briefcase and shouted, "Fine. You win. You always win!" She grabbed her purse and rushed out of the courtroom before she made a bigger spectacle of herself.

It just wasn't right. Her father was an awful human being, but things kept coming up roses for him. She wanted Nelson Marshall to pay for leaving her mother and ruining the family unit that she, her mother and brother had held dear. She had been a Daddy's girl, wanting to be just like Judge Nelson Marshall, for she had imagined that there was no greater human on earth than her dad. But that was before her father left her mother for Jasmine, her ex-friend, the skank. As a matter of fact, Jasmine had been Joy's roommate and her father had met Jasmine when Joy brought her over to the house for Sunday dinner.

As Joy reached the exit door, her head swiveled to the left as she spotted Jasmine seated in the last row of the courtroom. The woman had the audacity to roll her eyes at Joy as she looked her way. Joy wanted to reach across that aisle and go upside her head, the same way her mother had done to Jasmine years ago. But she reminded herself that she was in a courthouse and could get arrested for doing something like that.

Joy pushed open the door and walked out of the courtroom, and had almost made it out of the building when she heard Lance hollering behind her.

"Hey Joy, wait up."

She turned and waited for him to catch up. When he was standing in front of her she said, "Make it quick, Lance. I have a ton on my plate today."

"What happened in there? I've never seen you so frazzled."

Feeling foolish, she looked down at her feet and then glanced towards the wall behind Lance. She didn't owe him an explanation for her behavior. He wanted her to recuse herself and she did. That's it, end of story.

When Joy didn't respond he asked, "Is there anything I can do to help?"

"Yeah," she said, regaining her voice. "You can stay out of my business." With that she turned and left the building.

2

Jeremiah 29:11

For I know the thoughts that I think toward you,
saith the Lord, thoughts of peace, and not of evil, to
give you an expected end.

"I just can't believe that I made a fool of myself like that today." Joy was seated at a table inside of the Hallelujah Cakes and Such Bakery that her mother, Carmella Marshall opened a year ago.

The bakery sold decadent cakes, donuts, brownies and any other sweet treat that Carmella could think of, all freshly baked and served within hours of coming out of the oven. Since firing Joy and sending her back to law school, Carmella had gained ten other employees. Each of her employees loved baking just as much as Carmella did. They had all worked hard to make her growing business a big hit in the neighborhood.

Carmella handed her daughter a warm wheat donut with a cold glass of milk as she sat back down at the table with her. "You always let bitterness get the best of you where your father is concerned."

Joy dunked her donut in her milk and then took a bite. "It just makes me so mad that he gets away with everything."

"You let God deal with your father. You need to concern yourself with finding a husband and getting me a few grandchildren."

Coughing loudly, Joy almost hacked her delicious donut back up. She was finished with college, had been working in her field for almost two years now, and making strides as a prosecutor, but her mother's favorite question was still, 'when are you going to get married so you can give me some grandchildren?' But Joy wasn't even entertaining the thought of dating. Men simply weren't on her radar… they had been at one time. Joy had been engaged to be married five years ago. But after her father showed his true colors, Joy didn't know how she could ever trust another man. So she'd called off her wedding and hadn't so much as been on another date since. "Not interested, Mom."

"If you say so," Carmella said while giving her daughter the look of a doubting Thomas.

"What's that look supposed to mean?"

"I'm not saying anything." Carmella held her lips together and locked them with an imaginary key.

Joy could play that game, too. She put her hand up to her mother's mouth and unlocked her lips. "Spill it."

"Well, if I was going to say something, I'd probably mention that defense lawyer you mention every time you have a case against him. And if I had to guess, I'd say you're probably more upset about not being able to spar with that Lance Bryant, than you are about what happened with your dad."

"Mom." Joy's mouth hung open. "Why would you even say something like that? I have no interest in Lance or any other man, for that matter."

Carmella held her hands up. "Hey, I'm just saying."

"Mom, you have to stop this. Just because you found love again with Ramsey, doesn't mean that everyone wants to get married."

Just as Carmella opened her mouth to respond to her daughter, the door swung open. Carmella looked toward the checkout counter to make sure that Sylvia, her part-time afternoon clerk was standing behind the counter, prepared to serve the new arrival.

"What is she doing here?"

At the venom in her daughter's voice, Carmella swung her head back towards the door. "Dear Lord, and all the disciples except Judas, give me strength," was all Carmella could say as Jasmine Walker strutted over to their table like she had stock in the place, and was about ready to demand that they get back to work, so they could make her money grow. Five years ago, Carmella had beat this woman like she'd stolen something, because she had... she'd stolen Carmella's husband. Most days, Carmella was over it, and had no desire to fight over her ex-husband, especially since she had now been married to her wonderful new husband for the past two years. But Jasmine might not want to test her.

"I knew you'd be here," Jasmine said as she walked over to the table, glaring and waving her finger at Joy. "I need to talk to you."

"And people in Hell need ice water, but from what I hear, they're still thirsty." Joy wasn't about to waste another second of her life on a scallywag like Jasmine. The woman had befriended her, just so she could get her hooks into her father. Joy now questioned the motives of anyone who tried to befriend her. She had become closed off and unapproachable and Joy blamed the woman standing in front of her for that.

"Who do you think you are?" Jasmine demanded. "I'm tired of you treating Nelson like he's some sort of pariah. He is your father and he deserves respect."

When Joy didn't respond, but rather sat there staring at Jasmine as if she was two seconds away from going to jail for assault, Jasmine ignored the warning signs and continued on. "Fine, if you want to continue disrespecting your father like a two year old, that's your problem. But what you won't ever do again is disrespect him in his own courtroom. Because if you try to get him kicked off of one of his cases again, I'll file so many complaints against you that you'll be begging for traffic court cases by the time I'm done with you."

"Don't you come in here threatening my daughter. Haven't you already done enough to this family?" Carmella's blood was boiling as she popped out of her seat and got in Jasmine's face.

Jasmine backed up a bit. "If you touch me, I'll have you arrested."

Joy stood and grabbed her mother's arm, pulling her back into her seat. "I got this, Mama... wouldn't want you to break a nail on this unworthy piece of trash."

"Call me all the names you want, Joy. But I'm not playing with you. Nelson has lost a lot of money behind the outrageous alimony and child support your mother demanded of him, so I'm not going to stand by and let you cause him to lose another dime. Not now that he is finally through with alimony and child support."

The alimony had stopped three years ago, when Carmella married Ramsey, the love of her life. But she had received child support for Dontae until six months ago, when Dontae graduated college and got drafted into the NFL.

"I know you don't want another beat down, so what on earth could have possessed you to come to my mother's place of business and bother us?" Joy asked as she stepped in front of Carmella. Her mother had rededicated her life to Christ since she'd given Jasmine the beat down she deserved, but by the look on her mother's face, Joy wasn't so sure that Carmella Marshall-Thomas wouldn't be willing to go a few more rounds.

Jasmine swung her Gucci bag onto her shoulder, and put her hand on her hip as she told Joy. "I just don't like the way you've been treating your father."

"What were you doing in the courtroom, anyway? Did he call you for moral support or something?"

"Nelson and I had lunch plans until you ruined his day with your pettiness. You really need to grow up."

"Get out of here, Jasmine. How I treat Nelson Marshall," she refused to call him her father, "is none of your business."

"I beg to differ. As Nelson's wife, everything that affects him, affects me."

"Well, since you're not his wife, then it's like I said before… none of your business."

Jasmine lifted her ring finger and declared. "We're engaged, and we will soon be married, you can bet on that."

Joy waved a hand in the air, dismissing Jasmine. "Get real. It's been five years. If he hasn't married you by now, I can guarantee you that Mr. Marshall has figured out that he made the biggest mistake of his life when he left his wife for you."

"That's not true," Jasmine yelled and started wagging her bony finger in Carmella's direction. "Nelson has been afraid to get married since your mother stole his money in the divorce. But things are getting back on track for us, so you'll be receiving our wedding invitation soon enough."

"Don't bother, I already have enough trash to throw away," Joy said with a smirk on her face.

Another customer walked into the bakery, glanced over at the three women and then hesitated for a moment, as if she was unsure if she'd entered a safe environment.

Carmella waved the woman in. "Come on in, Betty, Sylvia has your order packed and waiting for you at the register."

"Oh, okay," the woman said, but still appeared nervous as she headed towards the checkout counter.

Jasmine opened her mouth to say something else, but Carmella shushed her. Betty paid for her baked goods and then rushed out the door as fast as she could. Once her customer had left, Carmella went to the door, opened it and pointed toward the cool outside air. "Get out. And please refrain from bringing your drama to my place of business in the future."

Jasmine rocked her hips as she strutted towards the door. "Do you think I keep a figure like this by hanging out in donut shops?"

Carmella wanted to yell at her to get it right. She didn't own a donut shop. Her bakery was high-end and supplied its customers with all sorts of tasty treats. But she didn't want to waste any more lung activity on her. She was too busy silently praying for

the Lord to stop her from acting on her fleshly desires
—hitting Jasmine until blood gushed out of her head.

"Leave my man alone," was Jasmine's finally
parting shot as she left the building.

Carmella closed the door behind her and
exhaled. "Whew, I barely passed that test. I need to
turn on my praise music and get my mind right after
dealing with that woman." Carmella walked behind
the counter, and switched on her CD player. Kirk
Franklin's *Smile* was playing. Carmella popped her
fingers and danced back to the table where she had
been sitting with her daughter.

Joy looked despondent as she said, "See that's
the difference between you and me. I've been so
angry about the whole situation that I couldn't praise
God if I wanted to."

Carmella gently put her hand on her daughter's
shoulder. "Honey, I know that things didn't turn out
the way you dreamed they would. But God didn't do
this to us. Nelson chose to leave of his own free will.
And you know what?"

"What?" Joy reluctantly asked.

"I spent a lot of time in prayer asking God to
give me the kind of heart that forgives. And one day,
as I was praising the Lord, I realized that I wasn't
angry with Nelson anymore."

"How long did it take you to get to that point?"

Carmella answered honestly. "About two and a
half years. Once I freed myself from the bondage of

unforgiveness the situation with your father had put me in, I was then free to marry Ramsey."

"But Ramsey would have married you much sooner than that, Mom. I talked to him... he was ready from day one."

"Yeah, but I didn't want to bring bitterness into our marriage. That wouldn't have been fair to him. I love Ramsey too much for that."

Joy nodded as she put her hand to her heart. "I'm happy for you and Ramsey, Mom. I really am. But I don't think I'll ever find love again. I know you think that I'm just bitter, and I can admit that I am. I don't know how to get past this barrier that has me so full of hate."

"Can you take some advice from your old mom?"

Joy grinned. "Of course I can. You know I value your opinion."

"Start praying again. Talk to God about how you're feeling and what's troubling you. And in the midst of all of that, you'll begin to sing a new song of praise... I guarantee it."

Joy shook her head. "If I tried talking to God it would probably come out as a bunch of angry questions."

"And that would be a good start," Carmella told her daughter.

"Mom, come on. All I heard since I was a child was how God was sovereign. He could do what he wanted to do, and we couldn't question Him about any of it."

"Oh really," Carmella said as she leaned back and studied her child. "So do you think that Daniel never had a question for God when he was thrown into the lion's den, or the three Hebrew boys when they were thrown into the fiery furnace? What about King David, when he and his men came back from battle and discovered that their families had been captured and taken from them? How about Apostles Peter and Paul... all that time they spent in service to God and what was the thanks they got for it? Prison and death. Do you think they never questioned God?"

Joy raised a hand. "Okay Mom, I get your point. Bad things have happened to a great deal of people who have gone on to serve God anyhow."

"That is correct. But what I'm really trying to get you to understand is that we are all human. Sometimes we question the wisdom of God for allowing certain things to occur, because we can't see the future and we don't always understand that better days are ahead. So, if your prayers start off as questions to God, go ahead. Asking those questions might just be the loudest praise song you'll ever sing. As far as I'm concerned, it's just praise in disguise."

"How can my questioning God be considered praise?" Joy was confused about the concept.

"Going to God in the first place, is your acknowledgment of who He is in your life. So go on and ask your questions... praise Him in disguise, and see if you won't get your answers."

Joy kissed her mother on the cheek and stood. "I've got to get back to work. Next time I stop in for lunch, at least have a turkey sandwich or something in this place."

"This is a bakery, Joy. You'll have to bring your own sandwiches and bring one for your mother, also."

As Joy headed towards the door *Are You Listening* began playing. Joy put her hand on the doorknob, but didn't move. Carmella could tell the words of that song were affecting her. Numerous big name gospel singers were involved in the album that Kirk Franklin had produced for Haiti. None of the singers mattered at that moment, only the words.

Paraphrasing the words, Carmella told her daughter, "Yes, Joy, God is listening, talk to Him, because He feels your pain."

3

Psalm 13: 1-2

How long wilt thou forget me, O Lord? For
ever? How long wilt thou hide thy face from me?
How long shall I take counsel in my soul, having
sorrow in my heart daily? How long shall mine
enemy be exalted over me?

When Carmella arrived home that night, Ramsey
was on the phone with Dontae. Carmella felt a twinge
of jealousy as she listened to her husband talk with
her son as if they were the best of friends. Oh, she
was thrilled that both her kids were over the moon
about Ramsey; that made her decision to remarry a
whole lot easier. She wanted her son to feel like he
could come to her with anything. But she realized his
need for a father figure and tried to calm her jealous
heart. She sat down on the sofa, picked up the remote
and turned the television to the evening news.

"I got you, man, don't even worry about it,"
Ramsey said as he and Dontae ended the call.

"What did Dontae want?" Carmella muted the television as Ramsey joined her on the sofa.

"Do you normally greet your man with questions or a kiss after a long day of work?"

She smiled. Ramsey was a wonderful husband... and the fact that he was so into her, didn't hurt matters one bit. Carmella threw her arms around him and lovingly kissed him. But as soon as they parted, she asked again, "What did Dontae want?"

Ramsey placed a kiss on her forehead. "He got us a box for his game against the Panthers and he made me promise that all of us would be there."

"But how can you make that promise? Only Joy, Renee and Ronny still live in North Carolina."

"Raven and Ramsey Jr. are only a plane ride away, but you are right about RaShan, he's still on his mission trip to Africa, so he won't be able to attend," Ramsey conceded.

All of Ramsey's children's names began with an 'R'. If that didn't signify just how much love was going on between him and his first wife, Carmella didn't know what would. Even though Carmella wished she had never let Ramsey go in the first place after having been high school sweethearts, she was still thankful that Ramsey's first wife had adored him. And she understood that a small part of Ramsey would always belong to his deceased wife.

Carmella didn't mind. Ramsey was able to love her and give his heart without worrying about what Carmella might do to him, because of the love relationship he had already experienced. Carmella, on the other hand, still dealt with insecurity issues because of the way Nelson had discarded her and she suspected that she would have those issues for some time to come. But Ramsey was patient with her. He recognized the baggage that Carmella brought into the marriage, so he was careful not to do things that stoked her insecurities like sneaking around or keeping secrets and Carmella was grateful for that. The Lord knew just what she needed in a forever partner since her first marriage had ended so horribly.

"It's important to Dontae that we all come to his game. He plans to treat us like royalty with our own box where we can watch the game and eat to our hearts' content."

"You did tell that boy not to order alcohol for us, right?" Carmella knew her son. He was in his partying stage and she wasn't about to put up with his shenanigans.

"He knows." Ramsey lifted Carmella's hands and held onto them as he added, "But hon, we need to talk, because there's something else you need to know."

His comment worried her, but it wasn't the kind of I'm-leaving-you-for-my-twenty-three-year-old-girlfriend worry that she had when Nelson wanted to talk. Her worry was that Dontae might have gotten himself into some other trouble, like the time he'd gotten arrested for busting out Jasmine's car windows or the time he'd been arrested for drunk driving two years ago, when he and his fellow college football players were out celebrating a win.

"He's not in any trouble, is he?"

Ramsey shook his head. "No, Carmella. It's nothing like that. This is good news. Dontae wants to introduce us to a lady friend of his."

Carmella's eyes got big. "My baby is serious about someone?"

Nodding, Ramsey said, "I think he is. And he's not your baby anymore. Dontae is a grown man and you're going to have to accept that."

"Grown man?" She rolled her eyes at that comment. "He's twenty-two, Ramsey. What boy do you know that is fully grown at twenty-two and able to make a decision about getting serious with a woman?"

"I was," Ramsey said with a hint of sadness in his eyes.

"Aw honey," Carmella said as she gently put her hand on Ramsey's face. "I'm sorry that things ended the way they did with your first marriage."

"Before you came along, I didn't think I would ever be happy again. I'm thankful that God reconnected us."

"So am I." They kissed again.

Then Ramsey said, "One more thing. And I need you to take a deep breath."

She did.

"Dontae wants Nelson to come to the game that night, also. And he really needs you to be okay with that."

Carmella took another deep breath. "Whew," she said as she fanned her face. "I didn't expect that. But then again, I guess I should have." She took another deep breath, calming herself. "Okay, if that's what Dontae wants, then I'll find a way to be all right with it."

"I'm anxious to meet this girl who has Dontae all tied up in knots," Ramsey said, trying to get the conversation away from Nelson.

"She better treat him right, that's all I have to say."

Ramsey shook a finger at her. "Carmella, be nice to this girl. It's important to Dontae."

Carmella lifted her hands. "Hey, as long as she knows how special Dontae is, she'll have no problems with me... what's her name?" Carmella asked, but then something on the television caught her eye. She picked up the remote and turned up the volume. Nelson was on the news, but he was in handcuffs.

"What's this about?" Ramsey asked as he turned his face toward the television.

They sat there listening as a newscaster reported that Nelson had just been arrested on charges of accepting bribes on some of the court cases he handled.

"What the devil?" Carmella said as her mouth hung open. Joy and Dontae had a hard enough time dealing with the demise of their parents' twenty-five-year marriage. How on earth would they deal with having a father in prison?

***

Joy was rubbing her hands together and inwardly dancing like no one was watching. Oh how the mighty have fallen, were the words that kept repeating themselves in her head as she rushed into the courtroom for her father's arraignment. Since her father was an elected official, the district attorney's office was bringing out the big guns, but she had begged for the second chair spot, and now she was running into the courtroom, anxious to see her father squirm.

But once again Joy's day was ruined by Lance Bryant. Evidently her father had hired Lance. The moment she walked into the courtroom, Lance and her father started whispering. When the judge took his seat and the arraignment began, Lance had the doggone nerve to say, "Judge Blake, I think we need to do a little house cleaning before we can begin this morning."

"What type of house cleaning?" Judge Blake asked.

Lance pointed towards the prosecution table. "Ms. Marshall is my client's daughter and we believe that she needs to recuse herself from this case."

"Recuse myself?" Joy said as if she'd never heard of the concept.

Lance wasn't above reminding her, however. He looked her way and said, "You do understand why you would need to do that, don't you? For the same reason you wanted my client to recuse himself... the relationship the two of you share as father and daughter presents a problem for the court."

"I am more than capable of doing my job. It doesn't matter who the defendant is. I can prosecute him just as well as I could any other criminal," Joy said emphatically.

Lance turned back to Judge Blake. "Assistant DA Joy Marshall has very strong feelings against her father since he divorced her mother. Therefore, we do not believe that she will be able to handle this case objectively. As a matter-of-fact, we don't understand why the DA's office would even allow a daughter to prosecute her own father."

I begged them for the second chair, that's why, Joy wanted to shout at Lance.

Assistant District Attorney Markus Gavin spoke up. "I am the first chair on this case, and I can get another attorney for my second chair, if that will solve the problem."

"No, Markus." Joy shook her head.

Markus turned to Joy. The look on his face was not sympathetic. "They're right, Joy. I never should have given you the second chair on this case. Let's just make this go away so we can get on with the case, okay?"

Joy wanted to object, throw herself on the mercy of the court… something… anything. But in the end, she knew she wasn't going to win the argument. So she yielded to the court. She caught the smirk on Lance's face, as if he thought he'd won against her again. She wanted to jump across the prosecution table and wipe that smirk off of his face.

After bail was set, Joy was still fuming, so before leaving the courtroom, she pulled up beside Lance, touched his arm to get his attention. When he turned toward her, she said, "I need to speak with you for a moment."

Lance turned to his client for approval. Nelson said, "Go ahead, I'll meet you in your office in about an hour." Then Nelson looked toward Joy and nodded. "Good to see you this morning, Joy."

"It wouldn't have been good for you if your lawyer hadn't had me thrown off the case. Are you afraid of your own daughter? Is that what this is about?" Joy fired back.

"I just didn't want you mixed up in this mess. I've damaged our relationship enough. I don't want one more thing to come between us."

"That's real sweet of you, Daddy dearest. But you can save it. I don't have any bail money for you."

"He already has his bail covered, but thanks for thinking about my client," Lance said as the guards took Nelson away.

"Don't try to be cute." Joy turned and stalked off. But when she noticed Lance wasn't following, she swung back around and said, "Are you coming?"

He pointed at his chest as if to ask, "Who, me?"

"Who else?" The man infuriated her. He acted all innocent, when he knew exactly what he was doing to her. Well, Joy wasn't putting up with his games anymore and she was going to let him have it. They made their way to an empty office on the same floor as the courtroom. The moment they walked in and Joy shut the door behind them, she got in his face. "Just what is your problem?"

"Wait a minute." Lance waved his hands as if waving a white flag. "Where's all this hostility coming from?"

"You know exactly where it's coming from. You keep getting me thrown off my cases. What's that about, huh?"

"Hey, you're the one who came into the courtroom the other day with guns blazing, trying to get your father thrown off a case. It just so happens that my client preferred your dad."

Joy wasn't listening to him. "And then you and my dad get me thrown off of a case I had to beg just to be allowed to sit second chair on."

"You had no business asking for this case in the first place. You know good and well that there is a conflict of interest here." Lance was not backing down.

"I also know that this is going to be a big deal case, and I could have used it as an opportunity for advancement, but you've ruined that for me now."

Lance stepped back and leaned against the door as he studied Joy without saying anything.

"What?" Joy said when Lance kept staring at her.

"I'm just wondering if the beautiful woman I spend my free time fantasizing about is truly as cold hearted as she seems."

Did he just say that he's been fantasizing about me? What was she supposed to say to that? Joy had no idea, so she chose to focus on the 'cold hearted' part of his statement. She folded her arms across her chest and said, "You stand by and watch your father try to destroy your mother, after he leaves her for your best friend and then come back and see me if your heart hasn't turned a little cold. I'd love to know how you do it."

He was staring at her without saying anything again.

"What's wrong with you? Say something, already."

"If you want to know what I'm thinking, I'll tell you." He pushed off from the door and sauntered toward her, prompting her to back further into the room. But he kept moving closer. "I'm glad that you've been recused from this case. Matter-of-fact, I'm going to ask that you be recused from all of my cases going forward."

He was standing so close to her that she could feel the heat pulsating off of him. Her voice got caught in her throat as she lifted her head, stared straight at those baby brown eyes of his and said, "I see no reason why I shouldn't go up against you on another case."

He lowered his head, and with their lips just inches apart he said, "I've got a reason for you." And then Lance dipped down, their lips met and he got acquainted with the taste of her mouth. When the kiss was over, the fire lingered, and Lance told her, "I wouldn't be able to do that if we were going up against each other on another case."

Joy couldn't think. Words were swimming around her head, but they weren't making sense. Her feelings were jumbled. She wanted to stepped away from Lance and give him a good dressing down for putting his soft, luscious lips on hers. But before she could make up her mind what she needed to do, the door to the small room opened and her boss, the district attorney peeked his head in. "I'd like to speak to you when you get a moment, Joy," he said without acknowledging the fact that she had practically been caught with lips locked with the enemy.

But Joy saw it in his eyes, and knew that the meeting she was about to have with the District Attorney would be nothing like the day he shook her hand, telling her she had a bright future with the department and welcomed her aboard.

4

Psalm 13:3-4

Consider and hear me, O Lord my God: lighten mine eyes, lest I sleep the sleep of death; Lest mine enemy say, I have prevailed against him; and those that trouble me rejoice when I am moved.

"I am so sick of this, Mom. I'm not just whining either. Some days I feel like I can't win for losing so I might as well just give up," Joy declared.

"It's not that bad, Joy. Please calm down," Carmella said as she sat in her kitchen with Joy.

"Not that bad? Mom, my boss just wrote me up. He said that my vendetta against Dad is clouding my judgment and making the office look bad."

Carmella handed her daughter a cup of hot chocolate. "So you just need to do your job and stop worrying about Nelson."

Joy rolled her eyes and then ran her hands down her face. "You act as if I want to feel this way. I can't help it, Mom. Just thinking of Dad and everything he did to us makes me see red. And now I'm going to lose my job."

"Stop being so dramatic, Joy. You are a good lawyer, so I doubt you'll lose your job over this. Just be careful and stop this vendetta you have against your father."

"I just get so angry every time I think about what he did to us."

Carmella put her hand over Joy's hand. "The divorce was hard for all of us. But I truly think you fared the worst in all of it. You were so busy taking care of me after I fell apart that you didn't have time to grieve or to deal with the loss of your hero."

Joy scoffed at that. "Some hero… the man is a felon."

"Your dad has done a lot of things, but I don't know if I believe he would take bribes. Nelson has too much respect for the law to do something like that."

Joy shook her head. "I don't understand you, Mom. The man left you for another woman and you are still defending him."

"After being married to someone as long as I was married to your father, I kind of think I know him a little bit."

"You didn't know that he was a cheater." When Joy saw the pained expression on her mother's face, she quickly said, "I shouldn't have said that. I'm sorry, Mom."

Carmella waved Joy's concern away. "Your father lost his way. I know that. But I once knew a man who was gentle and kind, and he loved God as much as I do. Now I don't know what happened to turn Nelson away from God, but I don't believe that he's gone so far that God can't snatch him back. That's why I'm still praying for his soul. So, I don't want you to give up on your father. Okay?"

Her mother was right. Her dad had been her hero. She had been a daddy's girl from the minute she was pushed out of the womb. Everything she did was about making her father proud. But he'd crushed her heart and spirit, and now Joy was still trying to put the pieces back together again. "I don't know if I can promise that, Mom. I think I've pretty much written him off. I'm even anxious to attend his sentencing."

"I hope you don't mean that, Joy. Nelson may have done a lot of wrong, but he loves you."

Unyielding, Joy said, "I don't trust him… and I think he's as guilty as sin."

"Have you done what I asked you to do yet?"

Joy wracked her brain, but couldn't come up with anything that her mom had asked her to do. When Carmella first started her business, Joy had been assigned as the go-get-it girl. Her mother would need flour or cream cheese or baking pans and Joy would run to the store and go get the stuff. But she hadn't been called on to do any of that in a long while. "I don't recall that you asked me to do anything."

42

"Joy, don't you remember that I asked you to start talking to God about some of the things that have been bothering you?"

"Oh… yeah, I remember you saying that asking questions of God might be the loudest praise song I've ever sung. And believe me, Mom, your words touched me. But I still don't see what good talking to God is going to do at this point in my life."

"Hold that thought," Carmella said as she got down from her kitchen stool and ran upstairs toward her bedroom. When she returned she was carrying a multi-colored journal. She handed the journal to Joy.

Joy looked at it. Three dancing women paraded about at the bottom of the front cover. The words, *When the Praises go up, the Blessings rain down*! were plastered at the top of the cover. "I just told you that I didn't want to talk to God. And now you want me to write to Him? I don't get it."

"You'll get it if you give it a try. I just simply want you to jot down how you're feeling. Tell God what hurts and why you are still so angry with your dad and with Him, for that matter. But then I also want you to take the time to tell God when something happens that makes you smile." Carmella stopped talking, took a deep breath and then continued. "What I'm hoping you'll discover from your self-examination, is that life really isn't that bad. And that God has given you plenty of good days."

"My life is going just fine, Mom. You act as if I need to be placed on suicide watch or something."

Joy didn't understand why her mother was always harping on her about this. She had done pretty well for herself... hadn't she gone back to law school and finished, just as her mother had asked her to do? She had even been moving up the ladder in the DA's office—that is, until she managed to get her first verbal warning.

"Your professional life is fine, for now. But the God-centered life you used to have is dead, and I'm just trying to help you resurrect it." Carmella pointed at the journal. "Will you do this for me? I promise you, if you give it a try, God will show up for you. And your eyes will begin to open to other possibilities as well... like the possibility of a loving relationship, maybe even with Lance Bryant. I mean, the man did kiss you today, right?"

Joy blushed. She couldn't believe that she had opened her mouth and told her mother about kissing a man while she was supposed to be working. "Why do I tell you all of my business?" There was a joking tone to Joy's voice.

But there was no laughter in Carmella's voice as she answered, "I know exactly why you tell me everything... I'm the only one you trust."

Joy opened her mouth to deny that, but she couldn't think of anyone else that she had willingly let into her world. So she closed her mouth and let her mother finish the indictment.

"You refuse to make friends because of the way Jasmine betrayed you. You refuse to date or give love a try, because of the way your father treated me." Carmella put her arms around Joy, hugged her real tight as she added, "You're a grown woman, living on your own these days, but when I look at you I am reminded of that seven-year-old-girl who ran in the house after school one day and declared that she was never leaving the house again because the kids at school were too mean."

"Those kids were mean," Joy declared.

"Yeah, but you got over it. You kept going back to school and day by day, things got better for you. This is the same thing, Joy. And if you need to dig deep to find some strength from that seven year old you used to be, then that's what I need you to do."

That incident at school occurred a little over twenty years ago, but Joy still remembered how she'd run into the house and tried to hide under the covers on her bed. Her mother had come into the room, sat down on her bed and listened as Joy had cried and confessed to having a hard time in her new school. Carmella's ready answer had been prayer. Joy had gotten down on her knees that afternoon and prayed for all the mean girls. When she went back to school and the girls were still mean to her, Joy told her mother that prayer didn't work. But Carmella told her that she needed to keep on praying. Within a couple of weeks, the meanest girl, Sally something-or-other had gotten sick and was out of school for two weeks. Joy had asked her mom to take her to Sally's house so she could pray with the girl. They did that and when

Sally came back to school, she told everyone how nice Joy had been to her... problem solved.

"I just don't know if a seven year old's answers will work for my current problems."

"You'll never know, unless you give it a try. Just consider it your own little praise journal," Carmella told her.

Joy looked down at the journal in her hand and read the words on the cover again, *When the Praises go up, the Blessings rain down*! She didn't know about that, but maybe she did need a new outlet for telling all her business. Since she didn't have any friends outside of her mother, maybe this journal thing would work for her. "Okay, I'll do it."

***

When Joy arrived at work the next day, she went straight to Markus Gavin's office. Since Markus was the senior ADA, he had the ear of the District Attorney and she was quite sure that Markus was upset after she'd been thrown off her father's case. Markus probably felt that she'd made him look bad, so he'd ratted her out to the DA. When her boss first approached her about his concerns, Joy had been angry with Markus, but after hearing Lance, the DA and her mother tell her that she had no business on the case in the first place, she realized that she owed Markus an apology.

She knocked on his office door. Joy didn't have an office, just a cubicle, but she had no doubt that she would one day move up to her own office also... if she could get her act together as the DA told her to do.

"Come in," Markus said from inside the office.

Joy opened the door and stepped inside.

Markus immediately lifted a hand, halting her. "I don't want to hear it. You deserve whatever you got from the DA."

"Hey, I came in here to apologize to you, but if you don't want to hear it, fine. I'll just go back to my cubicle and get to work."

Markus leaned back in his seat, studying Joy. "You must have gotten chewed out pretty bad to be in here begging my pardon."

Markus was a good ADA, but he was a real jerk. "Nobody chewed me out." *Okay, she was lying about that.* "But after careful consideration, I realized that I shouldn't have been so anxious to be a part of a case against my father in the first place."

"Didn't you used to work in his office?"

Joy nodded. "While I was in law school."

"Did you notice any improprieties?"

"Everything was handled above board when I worked there. Never once heard anyone claim that their case had been fixed."

"Then why do you believe he's guilty?" Markus asked, still studying her.

Even as she said, "I have my reasons," Joy heard her mother declaring that her father wasn't guilty of the crime. And for one brief moment she felt ashamed that she wasn't even willing to give her own father the benefit of the doubt.

"Anyway, I just wanted to apologize." Joy rushed out of Markus' office and made her way back to her cubicle. She had been so sure that her father was guilty the day before, so why was she letting her mother's words get into her head and cause her to second guess herself? And why was Lance Bryant leaning against her cubicle, staring at her as if she was a strawberry that had been double dipped in chocolate. "What are you doing here?" she asked as she strode past him into her cubicle.

Lance followed her and sat down in the chair on the side of her desk. "I wanted to make sure you were all right."

Joy leaned over and lowered her voice as she said, "It wasn't good enough to get me thrown off of my father's case. I guess now you want to get me fired as well, huh?"

"Are you kidding? If I got you fired, your father would fire me. And plus, I doubt if you'd ever agree to have dinner with me if I got you fired," Lance said with a sheepish look on his face.

Joy wasn't in a playing mood. "What do you want, Lance?"

"Okay well, we can talk about the date later."

"I'm not going out on a date with you. You're defending my father and this office is prosecuting him." Lance was fine... she didn't know too many women who wouldn't be drooling over him, and some would ask him out themselves. But Joy wasn't about to get caught up in some man who would probably be cheating on her two seconds after she said, 'I do'.

"As I said, we can save the date for later," Lance persisted. "But I do need help with your father's case."

Joy forgot to whisper as she exploded. "Is this a joke? Are you and my father trying to play a little game of entrapment?"

Lance started waving his hands. "No Joy, you've got it all wrong. I wouldn't do that to you. I just think the DA's office is making a big mistake by prosecuting this case and I thought you'd like to do something about it."

"What would ever make you think a thing like that?" Lance had called her cold-hearted, but he didn't know the half of it. Her heart had iced over where her father was concerned.

"Nelson is your father, Joy," Lance said, as if reminding her of a neglected fact. "I would think that fact alone would at least earn him the benefit of the doubt."

"Well you thought wrong. This office didn't bring a frivolous case against your client. But if you believe so much in my father, then I suggest you prove us wrong, rather than asking me to do your job for you."

"You're wrong, Joy. And you owe your father more loyalty than this." Lance stood and walked out of her cubicle without so much as a glance backward.

Guess he no longer wants that date. Joy tried to pretend that Lance's dismissal didn't bother her, but in truth, it bothered her that anyone would try to act as if it was somehow her fault that her father might be a criminal. It was that *might* word that lingered in her brain. Joy was ready to pronounce her father guilty, but something kept nagging at her. She couldn't figure out what it was, but knew that she had missed something. When Joy turned her attention to her desk, she found herself staring at the journal her mother had given her. She was conflicted, so she decided to take the advice of the only person she trusted.

She opened the journal. At the top of the page a scripture from Proverbs 3:5, *Trust in the Lord with all thine heart; and lean not unto thine own understanding.* After reading those words, Joy wasn't just conflicted, she was angry. She wrote:

> *I used to trust that You could do anything. But how can I trust You anymore when You allowed my father to cheat on my mother and desert his family? And now I'm supposed to feel bad about thinking my father is guilty when he's the one who should be ashamed of himself.*
>
> *And why, oh why did you send Lance Bryant my way? That man is hot. He's too fine to resist.*

Did she really just say that while writing in her journal to God? And why was she writing to God in the first place? It wasn't as if He was listening to her anyway.

Her mother was the only one who still believed in fairy tales these days. Joy closed the journal and got back to the real world.

5

Three days had passed since Joy's first praise journal entry. In that time another person had come forward, claiming that he had paid her father for a not-guilty verdict. The only problem with this guy's claim was that he was behind bars while making it. The DA's office was trying to figure out if Nelson took the money and just didn't return the favor, or if the claim was false altogether. Since she'd worked for her father several years back, everyone was looking to her to provide answers. But what could she tell them? She never noticed any illegal activity going on when she worked in her father's office, but she didn't know the Nelson Marshall who'd recently been arrested.

At home that night, Joy opened the journal and began to write about how hurt she had been to find out that her father was no longer her hero. She no longer believed in fairy tales and happily ever after and Joy not only blamed her dad for that—she blamed God, also. And every word she wrote in that journal let the Lord know just how she felt. After she had written five letting-God-know-just-what-she-thought pages, Joy closed her journal and went to bed.

After putting all of her hurts and pains on paper the night before, Joy was feeling pretty stress free as she drove into work the next morning. But when she parked her car, got out and saw Jasmine walking towards her, her stress level crept back up. "What are you doing here? Do I need to get a restraining order against you or what?"

Swinging her red lamb skin Chanel handbag, Jasmine strutted closer. "Why would you want to get a restraining order against your stepmom?"

"You are not my stepmother, my friend or anything else, just stay away from me." Joy tightened her grip on her briefcase and walked past Jasmine.

"Don't walk away from me, Joy. I wouldn't be here if I didn't need to talk to you." Jasmine caught up with Joy. "Your dad needs you to be a character witness for him."

Joy stopped in her tracks, and just about spit the words, "My dad has no character," in Jasmine's face.

"Why are you so ungrateful? You never wanted for anything, because Nelson did everything for you. Now that he needs you, you're M. I. A."

"Why don't you be a character witness for him, Jasmine? You can go to court and tell the jury just how upstanding and honorable your boyfriend is. Then you can tell them how you pretended to be my friend so you could sleep with my father and steal him away from his family." Joy put her hands on the door to go into the building. She turned back to Jasmine and said, "If you continue to follow me, I'm going to have the security guards arrest you."

As Joy walked into the building, Jasmine held the door open and yelled, "We're going to have you subpoenaed, so you're going to have to testify one way or the other."

It infuriated Joy that Jasmine even had the nerve to come and ask her for anything after all that she had done to her. It had all happened a little over five years ago, but Joy still thought about it as though it had happened only yesterday... she couldn't make herself forget and she certainly couldn't forgive...

"You better be glad we're friends, Jasmine. Because I would have to charge you for making me carry this heavy headboard if we weren't," Joy put the headboard down and massaged her arm.

Jasmine Walker grinned. "You know I appreciate you, girl."

"Well, I would appreciate this mystery man of yours, if he showed up to do the heavy lifting."

Jasmine poked her bottom lip out. "He's at work, Joy. Come on, help me load this stuff on the truck, and I promise I'll make him take everything off the truck."

They picked up the headboard and made their way to the truck. "So, I'm finally going to meet this mystery man who swept you off your feet, but never bothered to pick you up for dates." Joy rolled her eyes. "I truly don't understand why you've kept on seeing him. For as long as I've known you, you've never let a guy treat you so cavalierly."

They placed the headboard in the truck, and then Jasmine said, "Well, he's made up for it now, hasn't he?"

"I don't know, Jasmine... renting is temporary. If he were really serious, he would have bought the house and bought a ring."

Jasmine put her arm around Joy's shoulder as they walked back into the house to get the rest of her things. "You'll see, Joy Marshall, my man loves me, and he's going to prove it to the world."

They packed all of Jasmine's bedroom furniture in the U-Haul truck, Jasmine jumped behind the wheel and Joy got in on the passenger's side. As they drove down the highway toward Jasmine's new home.

"We're here." Jasmine pulled the U-Haul truck into the driveway of a spacious two-story home.

Joy's eyes widened as she looked at the house. From the looks of the outer structure, Joy figured the house had to be at least four thousand square feet. "Are you sharing this place with another couple or something?"

Jasmine laughed. She then shook her head. "No, he likes to entertain, so we needed enough room to be able to host parties."

"You sound like my mother. She's always hosting one party or another for my dad. You need to go take some cooking lessons from her so you can really do your parties up right," Joy suggested.

"Girl, please, I don't plan to do any cooking. That's what caterers are for," Jasmine opened the truck door and got out. Joy opened her door and followed Jasmine into the house.

Standing in the foyer, Joy was once again struck by the expansiveness of the house. The white marble floors, spiral staircase and the upstairs balcony that overlooked the foyer—all gave the house a feel of importance, as if someone with stature and influence lived there. "How can your guy afford to rent a house like this?" She knew it was rude to ask, but the question was out of her mouth before she could stop herself.

"Girl, just help me get those boxes out of the truck and stop being so nosey," Jasmine said with a good-natured grin on her face.

"I just can't believe this place, Jasmine. Troy and I sure can't afford anything like this."

They headed back out to the truck. "Once the two of you put your money together," Jasmine said, "I'm sure you'll be able to afford something nice, so don't sweat it, Joy."

"Please. After we get married, we'll probably spend the next five to ten years paying off our student loans. After that, we'll be able to start saving for a house like this."

Jasmine pulled a box out of the back of the truck. "I'm trying not to think about my student loans. At least your parents paid most of your tuition. But what I didn't get in financial aid, I had to cover in student loans."

Joy grabbed a box, and as they walked back to the house, she said, "Yeah, just when I started feeling grateful about not having so much debt to pay back after college, I met Troy and it seems like his middle name is debt."

"See, if you would have listened to me, you would have hooked up with an older guy who'd already paid off his debt. That way he would be able to take care of you in style."

They set the boxes down in the foyer and as they turned to go get more, Joy said, "I'm happy with Troy. Besides, my father had a lot of school debt when he married my mom, but they worked together and paid everything off. They're living pretty well now."

Jasmine didn't respond. She grabbed the next box and took it into the house. They followed that same process until all the boxes were unloaded.

Exhausted, they sat down on the floor next to the boxes. Joy said, "I don't think I want to be your friend anymore."

"I understand. I'm so tired; I don't want to move from this spot."

"I'm thirsty," Joy said.

"We have lemonade and iced tea in the fridge."

"I'll take the lemonade."

Jasmine stood. "I'll be right back. Do you need anything else?"

"A pillow. I'm about to crash." Joy pulled out her cell phone. "I'm going to have Troy come pick me up. Your man is taking too long."

"Suit yourself, but he should be here any minute." As if on cue, the doorbell rang. "Can you get that for me, Joy? I'm going to go get our drinks."

"Sure," Joy said. She got up and headed toward the front door. Before she could get to it, the doorbell rang *again, and then the person on the outside started pounding on the door. Joy was walking as fast as she could, so whoever was so anxious would have to wait. She was too tired to move any faster.*

By the time she got to the door, the doorbell rang for the third time. Joy was tempted to stand there a little longer and let the person on the other side of the door suffer a while longer. But when she looked through the peephole and saw her father, she immediately swung the door open.

As Nelson Marshall stepped into the house, he said, "I lost my key again."

Joy didn't hear him because as he was talking, she asked, "What are you doing here, Dad? Did Mom send you after me or something?"

Nelson swung around to face his daughter. His eyes widened. He stuttered, "Wh-what are y-you doing h-here?"

"I'm helping Jasmine move into her new house," Joy told her father. Then with a look of confusion on her face, she asked, "If you didn't know I was here, why did you come to Jasmine's house?"

Before Nelson could respond, Jasmine walked into the room carrying two glasses of lemonade. She handed one to Joy and then walked over to Nelson, kissed him, and then handed him the other glass. "You're late. What took you so long to get home?"

Nelson stepped back and turned toward his daughter. "I-I can explain."

But Joy was figuring things out all on her own. Jasmine's mystery man was her father, and the two of them had been sneaking around for over a year. "The person you need to explain something to is my mother," Joy declared, storming into the family room and grabbing her purse.

This was too much for Joy. Her father wasn't a cheater. He was a good man who went to work every day and attended church on Sundays with his family. But as she walked back into the entryway and saw the smirk on Jasmine's face, Joy began to believe what her eyes were telling her.

"You did this on purpose," Joy accused Jasmine. "You wanted me to know that my father was cheating on my mother."

Jasmine put her arm around Nelson and said, "It's time you knew the truth."

Nelson stepped away from Jasmine again. "This isn't how I wanted to tell her, Jasmine. You had no right bringing Joy here without letting me know."

Tearfully, Joy said, "What are you doing, Dad? This is going to break Mother's heart."

Nelson tried to put his arm around Joy. She pulled away. "Your mother already knows that I want a divorce. I'm surprised she didn't tell you."

Joy asked, "Why didn't you tell me? I spoke to you last night, but I don't recall you saying anything about divorcing my mother, so you could move in with someone young enough to be your daughter."

"I'm a grown woman," Jasmine said, "and Nelson and I are happy, despite our age difference."

Joy turned her back to Jasmine and held up her hand. "Don't speak to me ever again. I am not interested in anything you have to say." With that, Joy headed for the door.

"Don't go like this, baby-girl," her father said. "I really want to help you understand why I decided to leave your mother."

Joy opened the door and then shot back at her father, "Oh, I know exactly what was on your mind." She walked through the door and slammed it behind her. Joy was so angry that she wanted to hit something. She had looked up to her father almost to the point of worship for as long as she could remember. Nelson Marshall had been a man of integrity... someone she, her brother and her mother could count on.

Tears rolled down Joy's face as she walked away from her father's new home. She heard the door open behind her, but didn't stop or turn around to see who was coming after her. She wanted nothing to do with her so-called best friend or her dishonorable father.

What Jasmine and her father did, just about destroyed her. She'd lost faith and trust in everyone but her mom, and she'd eventually called off her wedding to Troy; a man who'd done nothing but love her. It hadn't been Troy's fault that Joy's father was a cheater. But he and Joy had paid the price for it just the same. Now he wanted a character witness, she'd sooner see him rot in prison.

6

Psalm 30:9-10

What profit is there in my blood, when I go down to
the pit? Shall the dust praise thee? Shall it declare thy
truth?
Hear, O Lord, and have mercy upon me; Lord, be
thou my helper.

Joy tried to go on about her day and ignore Jasmine's
comment. But the more she thought about it, the angrier
she became. She'd told Lance that she would do nothing to
help her father, and now Jasmine had the audacity to come
to her office and threaten to have her subpoenaed. By
lunch time, Joy decided that she'd had enough. Fuming,
she jumped in her car and drove to Lance Bryant's law
office.

Stepping out of the car, she checked her appearance in
the side view mirror. She loved the way her indigo blue
and tan wrap dress with the sash at the waist not only
looked professional, but felt feminine on her. He'd always
seemed to turn whenever she strutted into court with this

number on. She figured Lance would most likely drool all over himself when he saw her, but she couldn't care less. Joy was there to give him a piece of her mind and nothing more.

She'd never been to his law office before, but as she walked in, she found that she was impressed by how spacious and well decorated the waiting area was. Abstract art decorated the walls and dark, comfortably cushioned furniture greeted guests that entered the Bryant and Associates office building.

"May I help you?" A petite, older woman behind the receptionist desk asked.

"I'm here to see Lance Bryant."

"Do you have an appointment?"

"He wanted to talk with me about setting a date," Joy said without feeling the least bit troubled by stretching the truth.

"And your name?" the woman asked as she took off her glasses and picked up the phone.

"Tell him that Joy Marshall is here to see him."

The receptionist turned away from Joy and called Lance. All Joy could hear was the one sided conversation of, "yes", "that's fine", and "will do." She hung up the phone and then told Joy, "Mr. Bryant will be with you momentarily."

Joy sat down on the comfy looking sofa and proceeded to wait about fifteen minutes for Lance Bryant. She was just about to get up and leave his office, when he finally showed his face. Standing up, Joy told him, "I didn't make you wait this long when you brought yourself unannounced to my office."

"That's only because you didn't have a door to hide behind."

"So you admit that you kept me waiting on purpose?" Right hand was on her hip and she was getting ready to let her neck roll.

"I admit no such thing. I've been extremely busy putting out fires lately."

"As long as there are criminals, I'm sure you'll have no shortage of fires to put out."

Lance bowed before her. "I do try to do a good job for my clients who are always innocent until proven guilty."

Joy was enjoying her back and forth spar with Lance. But she was about to bring him down. "I'm sure you know that my father is guilty as sin, especially since another defendant who appeared in his court has come forward and admitted that he also bribed your client."

Glancing around the waiting room, Lance asked, "Would you like to step into my office so we can talk privately?"

Giving him an, I-got-your-number stare down, she said, "Oh, I thought you wanted to hold this little chit-chat in your waiting area. You certainly didn't make any mention of your office until your client's felonious activity came up."

Lance had been enjoying the light banter with Joy, too, but he didn't play when it came to his clients. With a look of seriousness on his face, he said, "If you'd like to discuss my client, I would prefer to do that in my office." He turned and headed towards his office.

Joy followed, but she was a bit taken aback by the fact that Lance had not looked at her with the same hungry eyes... the way he'd been caught looking at her on numerous occasions. He hadn't even noticed her dress—a dress that never failed to rein in compliments.

Lance seemed different towards her... uninterested was the word that came to mind. From the moment she'd gone up against Lance the first time, he had always given her that look. Joy had brushed off all of his advances, because she didn't want to date anyone. But now she wondered why she was so bothered by Lance's apparent lack of interest in her. Wasn't that what she wanted... to be left alone?

"Have a seat," Lance said as he closed the door behind them.

Glancing around his office, Joy was struck by some of the things she saw. He had the normal stuff: desk, chairs, sofa and work table, but on his credenza, there was also a statue of a man on bended knee with his hands steepled.

Noting where Joy was looking, Lance picked up his pint size statue and said, "This is just my little reminder that my clients need more than my skill as an attorney." He set the statue back down and added, "They also need my prayers."

Caught off guard by that comment, Joy couldn't help but say, "I wouldn't have pictured you as a church boy."

"I bet you wouldn't say that to my mama." There was laughter in Lance's voice as he added, "When I was a kid she bullied me unmercifully about going to church—said if I laid my head on her pillows every night, I could at least get up and go to church on Sunday."

Joy and her brother, Dontae had grown up in church, also. Her mother and father encouraged them to get involved at church, but she didn't recall any bullying. "Didn't that make you mad?"

Lance nodded. "I did get upset a time or two when I was a teenager. But I thank God that my parents followed the words in Proverbs where it admonishes parents to *Train up your child in the way he should go, and when he is old he will not depart from it.*"

Joy didn't believe a word he said, and just about accused him of being a liar with the way she asked, "So you're telling me that you never strayed away from God… not even while you were in college?"

Leaning against the credenza with his arms folded across his chest, he smiled at her. "I'd be lying if I told you that."

Joy didn't know how he did it. But standing there smiling, with those dimples dipping into his caramel cheeks, he transformed from a person she wanted to hate, to a man she could see herself loving.

"I strayed away from everything God and my Mama taught me when I was in college," Lance continued, "but after a few hard knocks, I got my head together and went running back to the good Lord."

Joy wasn't planning to run back anytime soon. Her family had fallen apart and God hadn't done anything to stop it from happening. Since she was a little girl, Joy had always believed that God could do anything... change people, make them better. But her father had only gotten worse. How was she ever supposed to trust God with anything after that?

"Joy, are you okay?"

"Huh? Yeah sure, I'm fine."

"Where did you go? You got this faraway look on your face."

Joy rubbed her hand down her face and plastered on a smile. "Your comment caused me to think about something." And then to change the subject, she pointed toward the same credenza, which also held a replica of a boxing ring with two boxing figures who looked beat down, worn out and ready to throw in the towel. "I suppose you're a boxing fan?"

"Not really. I'm more of a football fan."

"Then why do you have this replica of a boxing match in your office? Does this depict any particular boxer?" Joy couldn't help herself, she had gone there to give Lance a piece of her mind, but she had to admit, she was curious about the man.

Lance nodded. "Mohammad Ali is one of the boxers in the ring."

She pointed at the boxing replica and began jumping up and down as if she was on Family Feud and had the twenty thousand dollar answer. "Is it the Rumble in the Jungle?"

With an impressed look on his face, Lance asked, "What you know about the Ali and George Foreman fight?"

"Unlike you, my father is actually a boxing fanatic. When I was a kid, we'd spend Saturday afternoons watching old boxing matches."

"My father is a boxing fan, too. Matter of fact, when I opened my law office, he came to my office and put that boxing ring on my credenza, and then he sat down and reminded me of something that I think about every time I'm about ready to throw in the towel and give up on a case."

"I'm all ears," Joy told him as she waited for him to continue.

Smiling ruefully, Lance said, "I can't let you in on all my secrets."

She turned back towards the boxing match, trying to pull the message out of it. At that moment she realized that if it wasn't the Rumble in the Jungle, then it had to be, "Thrilla-in-Manila, the match between Ali and Joe Frazier." Lance acknowledged that she was right, and then Joy said, "I know what your father told you, because mine told me the same thing years ago."

"I'm all ears," Lance said, mimicking her earlier statement.

"He reminded you about the last seconds in that fight. Joe Frazier's trainer told him to quit, but Frazier said no. Meanwhile Mohammad Ali was on the other side of the ring telling his trainer that he wanted to quit. His trainer hesitated and then Frazier's trainer called off the match, because he was afraid that Frazier might die if he continued. A lot of people think Frazier would have won if his trainer had just waited another second."

"So, what's the moral of the story?" Lance asked, wondering if he was standing in front of a kindred spirit.

"Pay attention to your opponent and never be the first one to blink."

Lance smiled, and then he snuck in a right hook. "I take it that you and your father spent a lot of time together? I was told that the two of you were once very close."

That caught her off guard. Joy hadn't meant to reveal anything of the relationship she once had with her father, but the boxing ring had taken her back... had reminded her of a father who once cared about putting smiles on his children's faces. She was tired of thinking about her father... tired of being reminded of things that no longer mattered. Joy pulled her purse strap up on her shoulder and said, "Look, I have to get back to work. I just came here to tell you that I am not interested in being a character witness for my father. You see, I don't believe he has any character. So, if you subpoena me, it will be to your client's detriment."

"Your father is very proud of you, Joy. He really wants to make amends for hurting you. I wish you would give him a chance."

Lance looked so sincere that Joy almost thought her decision mattered to him. But he would be disappointed. "That won't be happening any time soon, so I suggest you tell your client and his girlfriend to leave me alone."

Lance reached out and touched Joy's arm. His eyes were full of compassion as he said, "I'm sorry that your father's infidelity hurt you."

At that moment, Joy wanted to lay her head on Lance's shoulder and let the tears fall. During her parents' divorce, her mother had been such a basket case, that Joy had to be strong for her. As the years went by, she became angrier and angrier about the situation, but she had never taken the time to just be sad. Maybe if she would just let a few tears fall, she would be able to move past all the pain.

"Have you ever thought about forgiving your father for his shortcomings?"

He almost had her singing Kumbayah with him. But Joy wasn't falling for it. Lance wanted her on the stand, being a character witness for her father. And there was no way that would ever happen. "Nice try, but I'm no amateur. I've gotten in the heads of my share of witnesses, also. Throw in the towel already, Counselor. You're going to lose this one." With that said, Joy turned and walked out of his office.

***

Lance couldn't throw in the towel. It wasn't in his nature. And he couldn't help but stand there and watch as Joy strutted out of his office. He'd played it cool when he greeted her when she first arrived, but he'd noticed that dress she was wearing and wondered if it was legal for a dress to cling to a woman's body like that. Her curves were in all the right places and if it wasn't for the fact that Lance had been trying to get Joy out of his mind, he probably would have asked her out again.

Joy was one of the finest women he'd seen in a long time, but she was also very damaged. Lance glanced over at the statue on his credenza and he did the only thing he knew to do… he prayed.

7

Psalm 13:5-6
But I have trusted in thy mercy; my heart shall rejoice in
thy salvation.
I will sing unto the Lord, because He hath dealt bountifully
with me.

They traveled from Raleigh to Charlotte for the football game. Joy arrived at the stadium with Renee and Raven, her stepsisters. The two women were twenty-four and twenty-five, respectively. Joy always enjoyed herself whenever they hung out, but she'd never been able to relax and be comfortable in their presence. When her mother had mentioned Dontae's football game, she made Joy promise to have fun, and that's exactly what she planned to do.

"Renee, girl, you must be trying to catch yourself a baller with that short skirt you're styling tonight," Joy said as she watched her young sister strut her stuff in four-inch heels and a three-inch skirt.

"You better know it," Renee said as she swiveled around so her sisters could check her out. "Dontae better not play me today. We're at the game in style sitting up in these box seats, so he better bring some of his teammates up here after the game."

"And if he does, what are you planning to do with Dontae's friends?" Ramsey asked as he and Carmella appeared in the open doorway.

"Daddy, leave Renee alone. If she wants to snag a rich husband, I say go for it," Raven said. She wasn't as scantily dressed as her sister, but her style was showing through with the cute little silk sundress she sported. No high heels, just flip flops... the two sisters couldn't have been more different in their style of dress.

"That's my baby-girl; I'll never leave her alone. Not even when she's been married for twenty-five years," Ramsey declared.

"Thank God I'm not the baby-girl," Raven said.

"Oh, the same goes for you," Carmella told her jokingly. "I've seen how protective Ramsey is over you girls. So, just make sure you're on your best behavior tonight."

"That includes you, too, Joy." Ramsey hugged her and then added, "I know you don't get out much because you work so hard, so I want you to have fun tonight." He then squinted his eyes and leaned forward until their foreheads were almost touching. "But I'm watching out for you, too."

"Leave these girls alone, Ramsey." Carmella grabbed his arm. "Come with me over to the food table. I want to see how the caterer set up everything. I might be able to get a few pointers from them."

"That's my wife, always thinking about business," Ramsey said as he allowed himself to be pulled away from the girls.

"Hey, I'm just trying to make us millionaires by the time you retire."

"Carmella, it will be another decade before I retire, so I'm going to need you to become a multi-millionaire in that timeframe. After being a principal for all these years, I'm going to need to rest my mind in Hawaii, Germany, France, and London."

"Don't forget about Italy and Paris... that's where I want to go," Carmella reminded him.

"Baby, I would take you around the world and back," Ramsey said just before kissing Carmella.

"Get a room already," Ramsey Jr. said as he and his younger brother, Ronny entered the box.

Ramsey, senior would not be deterred; he held onto Carmella, planted a kiss on her forehead and told the group. "I can kiss my woman anywhere and anytime I feel like it. I keep telling you, boy... that's the privilege of marriage. Get some of that in your life and then come talk to me."

Junior waved away that comment. "Go head on somewhere with that. I'm only twenty-seven," he said while popping his collar. "I'm too young to settle down."

The boys went over to where Joy and their two sisters were seated. "Hey, who invited our parents to the game?" Ronny asked.

"Tell me about it," Joy said. "I'll have to have a talk with Dontae. The next time he wants to hook us up with some box seats… no parents allowed.

The game had begun, but Joy wasn't paying it any attention, because the moment she said, 'no parents allowed' her father and his concubine stepped into the box.

Nelson walked over to Carmella and Ramsey, Jasmine was two steps behind him. There was sadness in Nelson's eyes at he looked at the way Ramsey held onto Carmella. Playing it off, he held out a hand to Ramsey and said, "Thanks for inviting us. I'm thrilled to be able to watch Dontae play ball with all of you."

"We are happy to have you. And more importantly, Dontae will be very happy that you're here," Ramsey told him as he stood about a foot taller than Nelson, in spirit and body.

"Yes, I'm thankful for that," Nelson said.

There was a bit of humbleness to Nelson that Carmella hadn't seen in a long time. She prayed that the Lord was working on his heart. "I'm glad you could join us tonight, Nelson." She looked to Jasmine who was standing behind him, looking everywhere but at them. "I hope you enjoy the game, Jasmine," was all Carmella said to her. She wasn't interested in lying, so she said as little as possible to the woman.

"I'm sure I will," Jasmine said as she grabbed hold of Nelson's hand. "Come on, Nelson. Let's take a seat so we can watch the game."

Nelson let her hand go. As he turned and walked away, he looked like a man who was already in prison, rather than one awaiting trial.

Joy stood up and stomped over to Carmella. "What are they doing here?" She demanded of her mother as she stood in front of her and Ramsey, with her back to her father.

Calmly, Carmella said, "I told you that your brother wanted all the family here tonight."

Crossing her arms over her chest in protest, Joy said, "You didn't tell me that Daddy was included."

"He is part of the family, Joy. And it's important to Dontae to have him here."

Joy couldn't care less how loud she was as she said, "I don't understand you, Mother. Doesn't it bother you that this man—" she swung around to point at her father, when out of the side of her eye she saw Lance entering the box. He was holding the arm of a beautiful Nia Long look alike with the same stylish short cut and voluptuous body that Nia Long is famous for. The fashionista had on a pair of thirteen-hundred dollar Bianca Spikes with the red outer sole by Christian Louboutin. Joy knew how much the shoes cost, because she had been stalking them online, waiting for a pair to show up on eBay so that she would be able to afford them on her Assistant DA salary.

"Thank you for showing me to our box," the fashionista said to Lance as she let go of his arm and strutted into the box and down to the front where she promptly took the front row seat as if this was her world and everyone else was blessed to have her in it. "Who does she think she is?" Joy mumbled, but inwardly she was also asking herself who the woman was to Lance.

"I think that's her," Carmella whispered to Ramsey.

Joy turned back toward them and asked, "You know her?"

"I think she's the woman Dontae has been dating. He wanted all of us to meet her tonight," Carmella said.

"Well, she doesn't seem all that interested in meeting us. The only person she even looked at was Lance Bryant and he isn't even a member of our family."

Carmella's head swiveled toward the handsome Boris Kodjoe-looking man who was standing in the entryway. "Is that the young man you work with?"

"I don't work with him, Mother. He is the defense attorney who is handling Dad's case, remember?"

"I think he's looking over here at you," Carmella said, "Let's go over there so you can introduce me to him."

"I'll pass. I'd rather go talk to the movie star who just walked in." Joy walked over to the mystery lady, curious to discover if she was Dontae's girlfriend or someone Lance was dating.

Joy sat down next to the woman and stuck out her hand. "Hi, I'm Joy. So, are you hanging with the family tonight?"

Instead of taking her hand, the woman reached out and hugged Joy. "Oh my goodness, you're just as beautiful as Dontae said."

Taken aback by the affectionate way in which this woman greeted her, Joy leaned away from her a bit as she said, "I'm sorry, but Dontae hasn't told me your name." *Or anything else about you*, Joy wanted to add but didn't. What was her brother up to?

"It's my fault," the woman said, "I should have introduced myself, but I was so anxious to get to my seat and watch Dontae play that I forgot my manners." Now she held out a hand to Joy, "My name is Tory Michaels. Dontae and I are dating."

"So you're the big surprise that Dontae had planned for all of us tonight?" Joy was starting to feel bad about the way she had approached Tory. She obviously was very important to Dontae for him to arrange a party of sorts, just so his family could meet her. Deep down Joy knew that she had been less than charitable towards Tory because Tory walked into the room with her hand on Lance. *But why did that bother her? Was she really falling for Lance Bryant?* No... Lance was the enemy, and he would stay that way if she had anything to say about it.

Dontae had the ball and he was running for a touchdown. So Joy turned her thoughts away from Lance and toward the field. Tory was on her feet, shouting, "Go Dontae, go... show 'em what you're made of."

"He can't hear you all the way up here, Tory," Joy told her.

"Touchdown!" Tory screamed her excitement, then as she tried to calm it down, she sat back down next to Joy. "I just get so excited when I watch him play. My Daddy used to play the game. Actually, the reason Dontae and I met in the first place is because I was loudly cheering his team during one of his first games with the Saints."

"Do you live in Louisiana?"

"Born and raised."

Joy was beginning to like this woman. She seemed interested in Dontae's career and was being supportive. Joy could roll with this... Her brother had someone to share his life with, and she was happy for him. "Come on Tory, let me introduce you to everyone."

The two women stood and Joy began taking Tory around the room, introducing her to everyone. Carmella and Ramsey hugged Tory, Raven asked if she could borrow her shoes, Ronny asked if he could have her number. They all laughed at that, because everyone knew Ronny was just joking. He and Dontae didn't grow up as brothers, but they had quickly formed a bond once Carmella and Ramsey married.

Ramsey Junior was laid back as usual with his one handed salute. But Renee took the cake. She pulled Tory to the side and asked, "I like athletes, too. Can you give me some pointers on how to land one of these players?"

"Girl, pay my little sister no mind," Joy said, without even giving a thought to the fact that she had just acknowledged Renee as her sister.

"Don't worry, Dontae already explained to me how colorful his family is," Tory said. She then pointed in Lance's direction and asked, "The man sitting with Lance, is that your dad?"

Joy had been avoiding that side of the room ever since her father and Jasmine walked in. She wasn't prepared to go over there and make nice, so she stalled by asking Tory, "How is it that you know Lance?"

Tory put her hand against her mouth as a low giggle escaped. "These shoes may look great, but I almost broke my neck trying to walk here in them. Lance caught me before I fell, and then allowed me to hold onto his arm once we realized we were headed in the same direction."

Joy glanced in Lance's direction. He was engrossed in conversation with her father. Nelson said something to him and then Lance leaned his head back and burst out laughing. They were a few feet away, but Joy could still see his dimples.

"He said that he works for your father," Tory continued.

"What, huh?" Joy hoped that she hadn't been caught staring at Lance. What was the matter with her? She needed to get her head back in the game. "Oh, yeah, he's dad's attorney. Come on, let me take you over there so you can meet Dontae's father."

"Oh, I didn't know that you and Dontae didn't have the same father." The look on Tory's face was one of confusion.

Joy said, "It's complicated." They walked over to her father and Joy made the introductions.

After the introductions, Lance stood up and said, "Can I speak to you for a moment, Joy?"

She wanted to say 'no' and then ask him not to bother her anymore. But Lance had been bringing out feelings that she had long ago suppressed. Joy needed to discover what kind of hold the man had on her. "Let's step into the hall." Joy walked away from everyone without looking back. She waited in the hall for Lance to join her.

When he came out into the hall, Lance took one look at Joy and asked, "Do you ever feel ashamed of the way you act?"

"Excuse me?" Joy thought Lance had wanted to talk to her about his feelings for her. She never imagined that she was going out there for a lecture.

"Well, your name is Joy, but I've never seen so much as a smile on your face since I met you."

"That's not fair. It's not my fault that my father makes me angry."

Lance wasn't letting her get around her issues. "What your father did to make you angry may not be your fault, but the way you've dealt with it certainly is. You won't even give your father a chance and all he wants is to be a part of your life."

Joy was simply tired of trying to make right what had gone so terribly wrong. She put her hands on her hips and came back with, "He has the woman he wanted in his life. She's always around... we can't have a family event without her showing up. He can't even go to work without her sitting in the courtroom stalking him."

"What are you talking about? Nelson didn't tell me that Jasmine sits in the courtroom while he's working."

"Didn't you see her that day I tried to get him recused from my case?"

Lance shook his head.

"Well she was there and she even came looking for me after court... she didn't appreciate that I was making her man look bad or some other nonsense like that."

"Go, Dontae, go," they heard Tory scream.

Joy imagined the look on Tory's face as she cheered Dontae on. Suddenly, she wished she had someone in her corner... someone to cheer her on. "If you're done telling me how awful I am, I think I'd like to go back in and watch my brother play."

Lance appeared to be a million miles away, thinking about something else. He looked back at her and said, "Okay, but can I ask you something first?"

Tory was still yelling, rooting Dontae towards another touchdown. Joy put her hands on her hips. "What?"

Before he could get a word out, Carmella scream, "Oh Lord Jesus, NO!"

From the sound of her mother's voice, Joy knew that whatever had just happened was all bad. She took her hands off her hips and stepped back into the box. Tory was holding her hands over her eyes and Carmella was on her knees with hands steepled. There were looks of shock all around the room as the announcer's voice streamed through the room. "Aw, folks. That had to hurt. I'm not sure if he's getting up from that."

Joy turned toward the field. Two big burly football players were getting up off the ground. Another player was still lying on the ground, holding the ball, but he wasn't moving. "Is that Dontae?" Joy asked.

Everyone just kept looking at the field. A stretcher arrived on the field.

Nelson jumped up and ran over to Carmella. He grabbed hold of her hand, pulling her off of her knees. "Come on, Carmella. We need to get down there and see about our son."

Carmella got up and followed behind Nelson as they made their way to the field.

Joy turned toward her stepfather and asked, "What is he talking about, Ramsey? What happened to Dontae?" Her voice was louder now... demanding an answer.

Ramsey walked over to Joy, putting his arm on her shoulder. "Calm down, Joy. He is going to be all right."

She backed away from Ramsey, shaking her head. "Don't tell me to calm down. What happened to my brother?" Joy's heart was beating fast. Dontae was being placed on a stretcher, but he still wasn't moving. She had experienced so many losses in her life that she just couldn't deal with one more sorrow... one more pain. If her brother didn't recover from the blow he'd just received, then Joy didn't know if she would recover.

Tory got out of her seat, an anxious look on her face. "I can't just sit here. I'm going down to the field to see what's going on with Dontae."

"That's a good idea," Ramsey said, trying to be the calming force in the room. "Why don't we all head on down, so we can figure out what's going on."

Everyone began filing out of the room. Joy took two deep breaths and followed behind Ramsey as they walked out of the room.

As Joy attempted to walk past him, Lance pulled her into his arms and held on tight. "I'm sorry this is happening, Joy. I will be praying for you and your brother."

Prayer... It sounded good, but when does it ever work? Joy was at her wits' end and trusting God just wasn't on her agenda.

8

Psalm 66:18-20

If I regard iniquity in my heart, the Lord will not hear me:
But verily God hath heard me; he hath attended to the voice of my prayer.
Blessed be God, which hath not turned away my prayer, nor his mercy from me.

Joy was beside herself as she sat in the hospital waiting for the doctor to come out and tell them how Dontae's surgery went. This was supposed to be a night filled with family and fun. But Dontae's concussion had ruined all of that. The doctors said the hit shook his brain and knocked him out cold for several minutes. But that hadn't been the worst of it. When Dontae finally came to and tried to stand up, the scream he let out as he grabbed hold of his knee and fell to the ground, told them that something was terribly wrong.

Her brother had gotten through high school and college with no injuries, but his first year playing pro ball had just landed him on an operating table. Joy was so worried that this knee injury was about to end her brother's career just as it was beginning, that she wasn't even thinking about the concussion he had suffered—that is, until the doctor came out after Dontae's surgery and put them on notice.

Carmella and Nelson stood in front of the surgeon, Joy and Tory were directly behind them with Ramsey in between, holding their hands. "I feel pretty good about the knee. He'll need rehabilitation, but I'm confident that Dontae should be walking on his own in about six to eight weeks."

The room erupted in cheers. Then Carmella said, "Oh thank God... thank God. So, everything is okay, then?"

"I didn't say that," the doctor began again.

"I thought you said that his knee would heal fine. What else is wrong?" Nelson demanded.

"The Cat scan we did shows that the hit Dontae took on the field today shook his brain in such a way that I doubt he'd be able to sustain another hit."

"So what are you saying?" Nelson asked with an edge to his voice.

"It means that Dontae has a decision to make," the doctor answered.

Carmella wanted to know, "When can we see him?"

"He's in the recovery room right now, but you should be able to see him in about an hour. However, because of the concussion I would advise that you make it a quick visit and then come back in the morning. He really needs his rest." After saying that, the doctor excused himself.

"I don't like the way he tried to insinuate that Dontae needs to quit football," Tory said with an exasperated look on her face.

"Well hon, tackling is part of the game of football and if one more tackle might bring irreparable harm to my son, then I seriously think he might need to find another career," Carmella said.

"What other kind of career do you expect him to get? Dontae is a football player and I can tell you right now that I am not marrying no pencil pusher," Tory declared with hands on hips for all to hear.

"Who said anything about marriage? The two of you are just dating... slow down," Joy said as she decided that she didn't like little Miss Fabulous after all.

Tory snapped open her purse and pulled out a ring that had a diamond on it that was so big, it appeared more gaudy than elegant. She put the diamond on her ring finger and declared. "I'm Dontae's fiancée. He wanted to wait and tell everyone tonight. But since he didn't get the chance, I'm serving notice that I will not allow anyone to go in Dontae's room and talk him out of being what he was created to be."

"Don't you care about my son's life at all?" Nelson spoke up.

"Of course she doesn't care," Joy interjected. "She's just like the skank you left Mama for. Don't you see the similarities?"

"Who you calling a skank?" Tory swung around to face Joy.

Jasmine popped up from her spot in the back. "Nelson, you need to tell your daughter to respect me."

"Just let it go, Jasmine. We have other things to deal with tonight," Nelson told her.

"I'm not going to let it go. I'm sick of your family thinking they can treat me any kind of way, and you just let them do it." She angrily swung her purse onto her shoulder. "I'm going back to the hotel. Are you coming or not?"

Nelson looked as if he was finally getting angry about what life had put him through and he wasn't about to take one more thing. He stalked over to Jasmine, grabbed hold of her arm and turned her to face him. "My son is facing the most trauma he's ever had to deal with. I need to be here to support him and I need you to support me. Can you do it or not?"

Joy turned to her mother and said, "I guess he's finally seeing her true colors."

"Stop it, Joy. Your father is worried about your brother. This is not the time or the place to act foolish."

"You are always taking up for him. Why do you do that, when you know as well as I do that he deserves everything he gets," Joy said to her mother.

Ramsey stepped in front of Carmella and took his turn trying to talk some sense into Joy. "Stop acting like a child, Joy. We need to find a way to help Dontae deal with the news the doctor just gave us. We don't have time for all the nastiness."

"Yeah, I need my mind together so I can uplift my man. I can't be spending time focusing on his evil sister,"

Tory said with as much venom in her voice as Joy had displayed earlier.

Jasmine apologized to Nelson and sat back down.

But Joy wasn't in the mood to apologize to nobody. Matter-of-fact, she didn't even want to be bothered with any of them for the rest of the night. "I'm out of here. Tell my brother I'll talk to him in the morning."

Carmella grabbed her daughter's arm. "No one said that you had to leave."

"You want me to be respectful to someone that I have lost all respect for. So the best thing for me to do is to just get out of here and let all y'all become one big happy family." Joy grabbed up her belongings and left the hospital in a huff.

Carmella was about to follow her, but Ramsey stopped her by saying, "Let her go, Carmella."

Carmella leaned her head against her husband's chest as a tear fell from her eyes. "She still hurting so much and I don't know how to help her."

"I know you don't want to hear this, baby, but we can't help Joy. We are just going to have to pray and trust God."

"Looks like we have a laundry list of things to pray for," Carmella told him.

Ramsey wasn't moved by the circumstances. He shrugged and said, "Then let's get started right now."

Getting herself on one accord with her husband, Carmella smiled up at him. This was the man of her dreams… her soulmate. She could get through anything with Ramsey by her side. Her children would be okay,

Carmella was sure of it, because she wasn't going to stop bombarding heaven on their behalves until it was so.

So much anger and bitterness filled Joy's heart as she left the hospital, that when she arrived at the hotel her family was staying at, she did something she hadn't done in over two years. She went to the hotel bar and ordered a drink. And then she ordered another and another.

On her third drink, Joy received a tap on her shoulder. She thought someone in her family had found her, so her eyes were rolling as she swiveled around in her chair. "What is it?"

"Dang," Lance said, "you're even a mean drunk. What in the world am I going to do with you?"

"Not now, Lance. I'm not in the mood."

"And you think I'm in the mood to watch you drink yourself under the table?"

Joy signaled the bartender and then turned back to Lance. "I hope you came over here to drink with me, because I'm in no mood to spar with you over anything tonight."

When the bartender approached, Lance lifted a hand. "The lady is finished drinking for the night."

The bartender nodded. Then Lance pulled his billfold out. "How much do we owe you?"

"I don't need you taking care of my bar tab. I'm a grown woman with a j.o.b." She opened her handbag, attempting to pull out her billfold, but the first thing she pulled out was her praise journal. Time stopped for a moment as Joy looked at the journal that her Mom gave her so that she could communicate with God. The very thought made her laugh. And the more she thought about what a joke the journal turned out to be, the more she laughed.

"What's so funny?" Lance asked as he handed the bartender two twenties.

Joy pointed at the journal and kept laughing. Nothing had gone right for her or her family since she'd started this little journal writing journey. It was a useless waste of time and she was going to tell her mother exactly that.

Lance picked up the journal and opened it to the first page. He read the words and then gawked at Joy.

"What?" she demanded, not even noticing that he had her journal in his hands.

"You think I'm hot… and way too fine." He was pointing at the words in the journal as he spoke.

"Give me that." Joy snatched her journal away from Lance and slammed it back on the bar. "You had no right to read my personal business."

"Looks like that journal is your and God's business. I've never tried writing my thoughts to God like that. How's that working for you?"

In answer, she lifted her glass. It had less than an ounce of her drink left in it. She turned the glass up and drank it down.

Lance took her purse out of her lap and picked up her journal. "Let's go. You've had enough."

"As I said before, I'm grown. I don't need you coming down here telling me what I've had enough of. I stopped listening to my daddy a long time ago, and I don't need no too-fine-for-his-own-good man to try to take his place." She was swaying in her seat with each word. At one point she almost fell off the seat, but caught herself and kept on talking.

"You're drunk, Joy. I'm taking you to your room so you can sleep it off. We'll talk in the morning." Lance put a hand on her arm and helped her get out of the chair.

"What do we need to talk about?" Joy asked as she allowed Lance to lead her away from the bar.

"I came to tell you something. But you're in no condition to discuss it tonight."

"What did you want to tell me?"

"It can wait." They got into the elevator. "What floor are you on?"

"Eight." Joy leaned against the back wall of the elevator and held out her hand. "Give me my purse so I can find my room key."

Lance handed it over, then pushed the number eight and stood back while the elevator doors closed.

As she searched through her purse, Joy began mumbling and angrily shifting things around. By the time they reached the eighth floor, Joy had found her key and stepped out of the elevator, but she was still mumbling.

"What are you over there mumbling about?" Lance asked as he helped her to her room.

"I'm just tired. I'm mad and I'm tired," she said as she stumbled around. "God just keeps letting all these things happen to me and my family and I'm tired of pretending it's okay."

They arrived at her door and Lance said, "I don't believe that God is letting things happen to you. Dontae's accident on the field today didn't occur because God has some secret vendetta against the Marshall family."

"Whatever," Joy said, and then struggled to get the key card in the slot. Lance took the card away from her and opened the door.

Lance handed Joy her journal. "Get some sleep, Joy. We'll talk about all of this tomorrow. Okay?"

She didn't respond to Lance. Joy stumbled into her room and closed the door behind her. Walking from the living room to the bedroom, Joy threw her journal and purse onto the sofa, lost her balance and then stubbed her toe on the coffee table. She then proceeded to blame God for hurting her toe.

"Why are You so against me? Why don't You ever help me with anything? I'm so tired of dealing with all the hurt and pain that I go through." Joy entered the bedroom and kicked off her shoes. "Everybody wants me to trust You, but trust You for what? You don't care… You don't ever do anything."

In her drunken state, Joy even told the Lord, "All You do is listen to prayers and then ignore them. I could do that job." As she thought about her father's betrayal and the injuries that could end her brother's career just as it was getting started, she got angry and then swung at the air as if trying to box with God. She lost her balance. Her legs left the ground, her butt landed on the bed, but she was in a free fall that she couldn't stop, so her head hit the headboard. It felt to her as if her brain had shifted and her body was spiraling down a vortex of some sort. Joy wondered if God had just won the fight, by giving her a concussion, just like her brother. Then she heard a voice speaking to her as if out of a whirlwind.

Who is this that questions me without knowledge? I have let you have your say, now prepare yourself while I ask a few questions of you.

Joy became frightened at the voice she was hearing. Somewhere within herself, she knew that the voice she was hearing was God's. Now she was wondering if she had gone too far, and if it was too late to take her words back?

Where were you when I laid the foundations of the earth? Declare, if you have understanding?

When Joy didn't respond, the Lord continued His questioning…

Where are the foundations fastened? Who laid the corner stone there of? Who caused the morning stars to sing together or all the sons of God to shout for joy? Have you ever commanded the morning or caused the dayspring to know its place?

She lifted her hands to her ears, trying to drown out the sounds of God letting her know just who He is, and who she was not. Hands over ears could not block out the booming voice of God.

Who do you think provides the raven his food when his young ones cry unto God? Who wakes you up in the morning? Who put the breath of life in your body? If you can do it all for yourself, then declare it.

Shall you that contend with the Almighty instruct Him? You that reprove God, can you give an answer for yourself?

What had she done? Who did she think she was to tell God that she could do His job? She was now terrified that because of her arrogance, she would die in this whirlwind and never see her family again. Suddenly, with the thought of losing her life, Joy realized that things weren't as awful as she kept telling herself they were.

She wanted to live and she wanted God to forgive her, so she said, "I cannot declare anything. I had no right to speak to You that way. I will put my hand over my mouth, because You are God all by yourself."

But the Lord wasn't finished and the whirlwind persisted. *Get yourself together and stand before Me, for I will demand answers of you. Do you cancel My judgments and condemn Me so that you can be righteous? Do you have an arm like God? Can you thunder with a voice like Mine? Deck yourself now with majesty and excellence; and array yourself with glory and beauty if you can."*

"I cannot do anything unless You allow it, Lord. Please forgive my foolish words and allow me to live with the knowledge of your greatness."

After humbling herself, Joy was released from the whirlwind and felt herself drifting downward. She opened her eyes and discovered that she was, once again, on the bed in her hotel room and her eyes were wide open. She had been so wrong to be angry with God, who provided for her every single day of her life. These last few years, she'd felt as if she had been placed in a barren land with no hope of finding the promised land. But at that time, in that moment, it didn't matter to Joy. She had found God in the midst of a whirlwind and she now knew that He was worthy of her praise.

With tears streaming down her face, she opened her mouth and began to sing a song that the choir used to sing at her mother's church when she was a child:

"I will sing a fruitful song, in a barren land. Although everything seems wrong, I will still sing a fruitful song…"

She kept singing those words over and over, trying to get them down in her spirit. She wasn't feeling the effects of alcohol anymore. She was feeling grateful that God had kept her alive all these years so she could come to terms with the fact that God deserved her praise… even when things in life weren't going the way she wanted them to go… praise Him anyhow. Just because He is God all by Himself.

She got off the bed and down on her knees. As she steepled her hands to pray, she was reminded of the figurine of a person praying in Lance's office, and wondered if Lance was praying for her at that same moment. It didn't matter, because she needed to go to God for herself. So, she began her prayer by thanking Him for who He was. And then she said, "I know I'm not a pleasant person to be around. I know that I have let bitterness get in my way, but I don't know how to let it go. Prove to me that I've been wrong about You… help me."

9

Psalm 137:5-6

If I forget thee, O Jerusalem, let my right hand forget her cunning.

If I do not remember thee, let my tongue cleave to the roof of my mouth; if I prefer not Jerusalem above my chief joy.

The events of the night before had tired Joy out. So it was 9:00 a.m. by the time she opened her eyes and her telephone was ringing. Joy reached up and grabbed the phone. "Hello," she said, her voice was groggy.

"Hey, I was just calling to check on you."

She recognized the deep, smooth voice immediately. It was Lance. "I'm much better. Thanks for calling."

"Actually, that's not the only reason I'm calling," Lance told her.

She wasn't thinking about sparring with Lance anymore, she was just happy that he even had her own his mind. "What can I do for you?"

"One of my college buddies invited me to attend his church this morning and I wanted to know if you'd like to go with me?"

Joy laughed. "If this is your way of trying to get me on a date, I've got to say that you're losing all cool points by taking me to a place that doesn't even charge admission."

Lance laughed also, then said, "Believe me, I'm not trying to weasel out of paying for a date. I just figured that since we are both in Charlotte, and away from our home churches, you might be in need of a place to worship this morning."

"To tell you the truth, I don't go to church when I'm home… haven't for a few years now. But I think I'd like to go this morning, thanks for thinking of me."

"Okay, be ready in thirty minutes. I'll drive."

"I'll meet you in the lobby," she said before they hung up and then Joy flipped the covers back and jumped out of bed. She jumped in the shower, threw on a sundress and then called her mother.

"Good morning, Joy. How are you doing?"

"Mom, I have a lot to tell you. But we can talk later. How is Dontae doing?"

"When we left last night, he was alert and just happy to be alive."

"He has a good attitude… at least you raised one of us right."

"Hey, I don't know where you got that idea, but I raised both of my children right," Carmella informed her oldest child.

"I just wanted to let you know that I'm going to church with Lance this morning and then I'll meet you over at the hospital."

"Well… well. Okay then, I'll see you at the hospital this afternoon."

Joy heard the surprise in her mother's voice, but chose not to comment on it. She wanted to wait until she could tell her mother the entire story of how God had finally answered some of her questions and how she'd willingly praised God.

She met Lance in the lobby and then they headed out. "What church are we going to?" she asked once they were seated in the car.

"Turning Points Ministries, it's right off of South Tryon."

"Okay." Joy leaned back in her seat and got comfortable for the ride.

Lance gave Joy a questioning glance, then asked, "You didn't have anything else to drink this morning, did you?"

Her eyebrows furrowed. Then she told him, "I almost forgot that I had been drinking last night. No, I didn't drink anything this morning. I am completely sober."

"Then what's got you so chill?"

"I can't tell you all my secrets," she said, because the last thing she wanted to do was tell Lance that she'd had an encounter with God the night before. Her mother would believe her— that was the kind of relationship they had— but she didn't want Lance to think that she'd lost her mind.

"I don't even want to know. I'm just glad to see that you're in a much better mood. You even smiled at me when you came downstairs."

Joy didn't say anything, but her lips formed a smile again.

As Lance continued driving, he said, "I better strike while the iron is hot. Do you remember when I told you that I wanted to talk to you about something?"

"Mmmhmm."

"Well, it's about your dad."

Her smile evaporated. "Come on, Lance. I was enjoying hanging out with you. Please don't ruin my day."

"This is important, Joy. Just hear me out, okay?"

She waved a hand in the air. "Go on."

"You got me to thinking when you said that Jasmine was always around and that she sits in on some of your father's cases. And that she was present for the case when my client asked for you to recuse yourself."

"You must really hate the fact that I'm in a good mood, because you're trying to bring me down by rehashing this stuff."

"No, no, no… Listen to me," Lance demanded. "It always bothered me that my client didn't want to delay his trial while another judge was located. I mean, he would be out on bail, so why would he care, right?"

Now Joy was listening. "That's the same thing I thought. But once my father got arrested for accepting bribes, I figured your client had probably paid him off, just like the others."

"I don't think so. Your father assured me that he's never spoken to any of the defendants outside of court and I believe him. But what if Jasmine has been talking to these defendants and getting them to give her money so that she can talk your dad into letting them off easy?"

"If he did what Jasmine wanted, he's still just as guilty," Joy said.

"But I don't think he knew that he was doing what she wanted. Let's look at the facts. Your father has a total of six accusers, but two of them are behind bars, so they obviously didn't get the outcome they paid for."

"So you're saying that Jasmine has been playing my father for a fool all these years, and he doesn't even know it?"

"That's exactly what I think," Lance said as he turned in to the office park area where Turning Points Ministries held service.

"Even if it's true, I don't know what you want me to do about it." She also didn't know if she wanted to do anything about it, but she didn't want Lance to think of her as cold hearted again, so she kept those thoughts to herself. "I'm off the case, remember?"

"Come on, Joy. This is your father we're talking about. When you go back to work, just talk with the DA, ask him to interview those witnesses again to see if you all missed anything."

Her eyes did a half roll and then she said, "I'll think about it." Then she pointed in Lance's face and sternly told him, "But I don't want you running to tell my father that I'm considering doing anything on his behalf."

Lance lifted his hands in surrender. "Okay, but I'm telling you, your father is innocent. I just need a little bit of help to prove it."

Joy did a full eye roll as she got out of the car. She didn't want to hear anything more about her father. It was the first time in years that she had gotten dressed for church on Sunday and she didn't want thoughts of Nelson Marshall to ruin that bit of progress.

As they entered the small church, they were greeted by smiling faces and warm hearted people. Joy was immediately drawn to the place. Turning Points Ministries was not in a traditional church building. It was located in a business district. A realty company was next door and other businesses were all around it. But Joy felt the spirit of God the moment she walked in the building and she had a feeling that all the surrounding businesses were being blessed of God, simply because of the presence of Turning Points Ministries.

The praise and worship team was small and mighty. Joy was immediately put at ease by the sound of worship coming out of the mouths of the three women at the front of the church. Sometimes tears would flow down their faces as they worshipped, and she could see the pain of longsuffering on the face of one of the worshippers, but she praised Him anyhow… just like her mother had done. And just as Joy was doing right then and there as she lifted her hands in praise to God and gave Him all the praise she had, even as tears streamed down her face, because she, too, had longsuffering issues.

Fred Lott, Jr. was the presiding pastor of Turning Points Ministries. He was a tall fair-skinned man with a heart of gold. He reminded her of Ramsey as he spoke lovingly about his wife and about members of his congregation.

He then told the congregation, "You were meant to be free, and today I'm going to show you how to get your freedom." He opened his Bible and flipped a few pages. "Turn with me to Luke, chapter thirteen. I'm going to begin reading at verse ten.

"And Jesus was teaching in one of the synagogues on the Sabbath. And behold, there was a woman which had a spirit of infirmity eighteen years, and was bowed together, and could in no wise lift up herself. And when Jesus saw her, he called her to him and said unto her, Woman thou art loosed from thine infirmity. And he laid his hands on her: and immediately she was made straight, and glorified God."

"And the ruler of the synagogue answered with indignation, because that Jesus had healed on the Sabbath day... The Lord then answered him and said, thou hypocrite, doth not each one of you on the Sabbath loose his ox from the stall, and lead him away to watering? And ought not this woman, being a daughter of Abraham, whom Satan hath bound lo, these eighteen years be loosed from this bond on the Sabbath day?"

Pastor Lott finished his Bible reading and then looked up at the congregation and said, "I want you all to understand that there are some things that have us bound and we can't get free from them of our own accord, because this thing is a work of the devil.

"The woman with the infirmity stayed bent over, unable to fix her situation for eighteen years because she kept trying to do it herself."

Joy tried to imagine what it must have felt like to have to walk everywhere bent over for eighteen years. It must have been awful for that woman.

Then Pastor Lott said, "You can easily see people's physical disabilities, but what about the spiritual ones... what has you bent over? Is it financial... marriage... family?"

Joy's hand pressed against her mouth as she tried to stifle an involuntary scream. Her mom had told her that bitterness was eating her alive and now it felt as if this pastor was preaching directly to her. She had been carrying the spirit of bitterness for five long years and it had her bowed so low that she couldn't raise herself up.

"I came here today to tell you to straighten up!" Pastor Lott's voice roared throughout the building. "You might have been dealing with things all your life, but you can let it go today. Some of you have been dealing with bitterness that you refuse to let go of, but I guarantee you, the minute you let it go, that's when your deliverance will come."

It was as if God had allowed this pastor to read the very thoughts and intent of her heart. By the end of the sermon, Joy was an emotional wreck, but she didn't know what to do about it. Pastor Lott's words sounded good in theory, but she had been carrying her bitterness for so long that she honestly didn't know what she would do without it. She'd finished law school, stopped drinking herself into a stupor, gotten herself hired on at the District Attorney's office… all to show her father that she didn't need him and could be successful even without him in her life. If she let her bitterness go, what would be her driving force?

As he closed the Bible and ended his message, Pastor Lott said, I'm feeling very strongly, that God wants me to pray for a few of you. You know what… we're a close-knit group. Why don't you all just come on up here and let's form a circle of prayer."

Joy had kept to herself for so long, that even though she knew that she was probably one of the people God wanted Pastor Lott to pray for, she never would have singled herself out and gone up to the altar. But now that Pastor Lott had asked for everyone to come, if she stayed in her seat, she would be singled out for that. So Joy grabbed hold of Lance's hand and joined the rest of the congregation as they formed their circle of prayer.

Pastor Lott said a general prayer for the group and then he began anointing the forehead of each person in the circle. As he touched them he said a quick prayer that seemed tailored to that person. The closer he got to Joy, the more worried she became, because if this man read her mail and looked into her innermost thoughts, he would know how truly wicked she had allowed herself to become.

Tears began to flow again and Joy couldn't stop them. She had allowed her father's sins to turn her into someone she never intended to become. She felt as if she'd been given a life sentence with no chance for parole. But then Pastor Lott touched her. And from the moment he placed his hand on her forehead, Joy felt a consuming fire ignite her from within.

Pastor Lott stepped back and looked at her for a moment. He closed his eyes as if listening to the voice of the Lord and then said, "God has loosed you, daughter. Walk in your freedom and never turn back to that thing that tried to bind you for a lifetime."

Joy felt every bit of the freedom that Pastor Lott had just declared God had given her. She lifted her hands and began praising God like never before. Her mom had been right all along. For it was through her questions and bitterness that she had found God and learned how to praise Him while waiting on her breakthrough. Her brother was still in the hospital, her father had left the family, but Joy could now see that even Nelson Marshall's actions couldn't destroy them. As long as they had God, she and her family could get through any storm.

10

Psalm 51:7-8

Purge me with hyssop, and I shall be clean: wash me,
and I shall be whiter than snow.

Make me to hear joy and gladness; that the bones
which thou hast broken may rejoice.

After church, Lance took her back to the hotel. They
said a long goodbye, as the hug he gave her lingered so
long that the smell of his cologne stayed with her even as
they parted. "I've got to head back to Raleigh. I want to
get a jump on my investigation, so I can get your father out
of this mess."

"My father should be grateful that you're on his case,
because I know for a fact that you're not going to throw in
the towel. You'll fight to the end on his behalf."

"True that."

She smiled at him, then said, "Thanks for inviting me
to church today, Lance. I can't tell you how much that
meant to me."

"You don't have to tell me. I can see it in your eyes." Lance lowered his head and lightly kissed Joy then backed away with his hands in the air. As if he needed to keep them in the air or he'd do something else with them. "I'll see you when you get back to Raleigh."

Joy nodded. She then got in a cab and headed for the hospital. Carmella was waiting for her when she arrived. She and Ramsey had just come out of Dontae's room and now her mother wanted answers.

"How was church?"

"Wonderful." Joy grabbed her mother's arms and swung around with her. "Pastor Lott preached just what I needed to hear. But Mom, you'll never believe what else happened... Last night, I had an encounter with God. You told me to question God, and He showed up when I needed Him most and let me know just who He is, and that encounter made all the difference."

"I'm so proud of you, hon. You look so happy and I'm thrilled to see that look on your face again."

"I feel..." Joy hesitated as she tried to put words to her feelings, "like that seven-year- old child that I used to be. The one who used to believe that God could do anything, but fail. That's how I feel."

Carmella lifted her hands and gave praise to God. Although her son had a traumatic brain injury, he was alive, and now she also knew that her daughter was not only alive, but born again. She was truly amazed by God. He was a wonder worker.

Joy gave Ramsey, Raven and Ronny a hug, they were all in the waiting room, taking turns going into Dontae's room. The doctor didn't want all of them crowding Dontae at one time and the family was trying to be respectful of that. Ramsey Jr. and Renee both had to fly back home to get ready for Monday morning meetings, but they'd both come back to the hospital early that morning before flying out.

Joy and her mom went into Dontae's room. His fiancée was already in the room along with her father. Joy was thankful that her brother wasn't going through the ordeal alone. It was good to have a supportive family. Especially now with Dontae's head and knee aching so badly that he kept moaning and alternately rubbing either his head or knee. Joy didn't know what else to do, so she started praying for him.

Dontae smiled at his sister. "What's gotten into you? I haven't heard you pray in years."

"I finally came back to my senses," she told her brother.

"I'm just happy that she's smiling again," Carmella said.

"I got my joy back, thank you very much. The only thing I'm worried about right now is my brother."

"No need to worry about Dontae, he's going to be just fine. Isn't that right, baby?" Tory interjected.

Dontae winced and then said, "That's right. I'm Superman."

"Well those big linebackers must be your kryptonite." Joy walked over to Dontae's bed and put her hands on the bedrail. "Please tell me that you're not thinking about going back on that field. I know that you love the game, but we love you more."

Tory rolled her eyes and folded her arms over her chest. She was acting ugly, but Joy ignored it. There were many days that she had acted just as ugly and her family put up with her behavior; so instead of telling her off, she was going to pray for Tory and also pray that Dontae opened his eyes. *Good Lord, what was her brother doing with a woman like that?*

Dontae put his hand over hers. "It's hard, Sis. This is all I've ever dreamed of doing. If I'm not a football player, then what am I?"

"Exactly!" Tory shouted as if someone had been talking to her.

"Let it go, Tory. This is my family. They have a right to be concerned about me."

"I know, baby," she said as she came to stand by his side. "I just don't want them talking you out of a career that you love so much, just because of a little bump on the head."

"He was out cold for several minutes," Carmella corrected.

"You and I already talked about this, Mom. I listened to everything the doctor said. So, my goal right now is to go through with the rehab on my knee and then I'll make my decision on whether or not to return to the NFL." He looked around the room, from Tory, to Joy, to his mother and father and then asked, "Can everybody live with that?"

Tory pursed her lips and then strutted back to her seat.

The others nodded their agreement and Nelson said, "We just want you happy and safe, Son. That's all."

"I know, Dad. And to tell you the truth, if this had to happen to me, I'm just glad that my family was here. I probably would have gone into a deep depression if I had to face this alone."

"You are never alone, Dontae. And don't you forget it," Carmella told her son. "We're not just here for the football player, we're here for you."

They visited for a little while longer, then Joy went to the waiting area and asked Raven to walk down to the cafeteria with her to get something to eat.

Ramsey popped up. "If you're going to be out of the room for a while, we're going in." Ronny stood up and joined his father.

"Y'all can have it. I don't think I can take much more of Miss Hollywood-Tory right now. I need a long break."

"Was she that bad?" Raven asked as they headed to the cafeteria.

Shaking her head, Joy told her stepsister, "I honestly don't understand how both my brother and my father, two very intelligent men, could be so easily duped by these blood-sucking women."

"Tell me about it," Raven agreed. "And meanwhile, women like us, who want to be a support to a good man... we sit on the shelf just waiting to be noticed."

Joy couldn't imagine that as beautiful as Raven was, that she had spent much time on any shelf. But life was strange, and anything could happen, because Joy had put her own self on the shelf to avoid the hurt and pain loving a man could bring. She'd seen firsthand how her mother had dissolved into almost nothing after her father had walked out on her. She didn't want to ever feel like that. But did that mean that she would never give love a try?

"I don't know," Joy said with a look of hope in her eyes. "Lately, I've been thinking about taking myself off the shelf and giving love another chance."

"Oh my goodness... you've met someone." Raven was so elated, that she hugged her stepsister.

Joy could hardly believe that she was telling her business to anyone other than her mother and her praise journal, but she also felt like letting her guard down and learning to trust people again. "You remember Lance Bryant? He was at the football game with my dad."

In the cafeteria, they picked up trays and began grabbing salads and sandwiches. Raven responded to Joy's comment about Lance, "How could I miss him? The man is hot."

"I hope Renee didn't notice," Joy joked.

"Girl please, my sister was too busy trying to get hooked up with a pro-baller."

Joy and Raven ate their food and sat in the cafeteria laughing and joking with each other. As they got up to put their trays over the trash can and head back up to be with the group, Nelson appeared.

He stood to the side of the room, looking Joy's way as if unsure of how to approach her. It was in that moment that her father seemed most vulnerable to her. Despite what he'd done to her mother, Joy knew that her father loved her, but she had denied him her love in order to make him pay for his decisions. Joy was thankful that God hadn't denied her His love because of all the bad decisions she had made.

Joy turned to Raven. "I'll meet you back upstairs in a little while. I need to talk to my dad."

Raven put her hand on Joy's shoulder. "Okay girl, I'll see you in a bit."

Joy silently prayed as she slow walked over to her Dad. She hadn't had a normal conversation with him in so long, that she honestly didn't know how to talk to him anymore. *Lord, be my guide.* "Hey," was her great conversation starter once she was standing in front of the man responsible for her being born and being a Marshall.

He pointed to one of the tables. "Would you like to have a seat with me for a moment?"

His voice was shaky as he asked, as if he wasn't so sure if she would agree to give her own father a few minutes of her time. And since she had denied him on other occasions, she understood his trepidation. "I think it's way past time for us to sit down and talk, don't you?"

Nelson nodded and then guided her over to a table in the back of the room. When they were seated, Nelson said, "First let me tell you how sorry I am for everything that I did. When I saw that picture of you with your face in the commode, throwing up, I just wanted to run to you... to save you."

"You wouldn't have been able to save me from any of the things I had to go through, Daddy. I couldn't even save myself. But I don't blame you for any of the things that I did to myself anymore."

When Joy said those words, her father exhaled like a weight too heavy to carry had just been removed from his shoulders. She was overcome with compassion for her father. Joy put her hand over his. "I'm so sorry for the way I've treated you."

Humbled and with his head low, Nelson said, "I deserved it."

Joy shook her head. "No, you didn't deserve what I did to you. I am your daughter and I should have been able to treat you respectfully. It took me a while but I finally figured out why I couldn't."

"Was it because I cheated with Jasmine? Someone who was supposed to be your best friend?"

"That's what I kept telling myself, but the truth of the matter is, I had made you my hero. When you fell down from the pedestal I'd put you on, it devastated me. But I found a new hero, and his name is Jesus Christ. So, now I can just let you be my dad and love you no matter what comes."

As Joy finished her statement, tears were brimming in Nelson's eyes. He reached over and grabbed hold of his daughter. After hugging her tightly, he said, "I've missed you so much."

She hadn't hugged her father in over five years. Joy had to admit that she had missed his touch... missed knowing that her father cared about what concerned her. Things would probably never be the same between them, but at least they would be better. "I've missed you, too, Daddy."

Nelson wiped his eyes and tried to get himself together. He cleared his throat and then told Joy. "I wanted to talk to you about what Lance told you this morning."

Joy cringed inwardly. She prayed that her father wasn't going to ask her to do anything illegal to help him out of the mess he'd gotten into by getting involved with Jasmine in the first place.

"Lance's theory might be right, but I don't want to get you involved."

She breathed a little easier and then asked, "Were *you* involved? I really need to know, Dad."

Nelson shook his head. "I wasn't. If Jasmine is the one who took those bribes on some of my cases, she never told me that she was doing it. I do recall that she began taking an interest in my cases a few years back."

"Jasmine is poison, Dad. I just don't know how you could have left Mom for someone like her."

Sadness shaded Nelson's eyes as he admitted, "I have a lot of regrets. But there are some decisions that you have to live with, no matter how much you wish you could turn back time and get a redo."

11

Psalm 30:4-5
Sing unto the Lord, O ye saints of His,
and give thanks at the remembrance of his holiness.
For his anger endureth but for a moment; in his
favour is life; weeping may endure for a night, but JOY
cometh in the morning.

Three months later...

"All rise. The case of Nelson Marshall and the state of North Carolina will come to order," said the bailiff.

The case against her father had begun and Joy had come full circle. She'd once declared that she would never be a character witness for her dad because he had no character. But there she was seated in the courtroom as she waited to be called on to testify about what she knew about her father's business practices. She could only testify about events that took place five years ago when she clerked for him. But Joy now counted it a privilege to be able to tell others about the good man her father had once been. She only wished that she had the opportunity to tell the court about the good man her father had become in the last few months.

Forgiveness goes along way, and when Joy opened her heart to forgive her father, Nelson found the strength to repent of his sins and return to the God he had once served. He was in court, prepared to deal with whatever judgment he received.

As promised, Lance went to work tearing apart the testimonies like a prize fighter. Each person who accused her father of taking a bribe from them, left the stand looking as if they were either confused or the biggest liars on God's green earth.

Then it was her turn. Joy put her right hand on the Bible and swore to tell the truth and nothing but the truth and then she sat down on the witness stand.

Lance looked down at his notes as Joy situated herself in her seat. He put his notepad down and sauntered over to the box where Joy sat watching him move toward her. Joy prayed that she would be able to concentrate with Lance standing in front of her. She could hardly believe that she'd told this man that she wasn't interested in dating him. What was she thinking?

"Ms. Nelson. Is it okay if I call you Joy?"

Call me anything you want, just as long as you call me tomorrow, was what Joy wanted to say, but this was no joking matter. Her father's life and career were at stake, so she needed to quit drooling over Lance and get serious. "Yes, you can call me Joy."

"Thank you," Lance said as he hesitated for a moment, looked toward the jury and then back at Joy. "Joy, can you please tell the jury who Nelson Marshall is to you?"

Joy glanced in Nelson's direction. He smiled at her and it warmed her heart. "He's my father."

"You work for the district attorney's office, right?"

She leaned forward, speaking into the microphone. "Yes I do."

"And when your father was arrested, you asked to sit second chair in order to help convict him, correct?"

Joy glanced at Markus. He looked as if he was about ready to pounce out of his chair and object to Lance's line of questioning. But he kept his seat, so Joy said, "Yes, I did."

"And why did you do such a thing, Ms. Nelson?"

She wanted to remind Lance that he had just asked for permission to call her Joy. But she knew exactly why he had decided to use her last name at that moment...to remind the jury that this was Nelson's daughter speaking. She refused to lie for her father or anyone else, so she answered truthfully. "I wanted the case because I believed that he was guilty."

Sounds of disbelief escaped the mouths of members of the jury and others in the courtroom.

Joy didn't know why Lance would ask her a question like that. If a man's own child believed he was guilty, then why shouldn't they.

But Lance didn't seem bothered by the reactions in the courtroom. He trodded on. "Do you still believe that your father is guilty of the crime he has been charged with?"

"No," was her simple answer while she prayed that he'd have some serious follow-up questions.

"No, huh," Lance repeated, and then took his time looking at each jury member, making sure they were paying attention. "And let me ask you something else, if I may. You used to work for your father. Can you tell the court how long ago you worked for him?"

"Five years ago."

"During the time that you worked in his office, had you ever seen anything that would cause you to believe that Judge Marshall was taking bribes?"

"Objection." Markus pointed towards Joy. "She was a law student at the time, so she only worked part-time as a clerk for her father. She couldn't possibly know everything that went on in that office."

"Your Honor, I'm only asking the defendant to testify to what she saw with her own two eyes. I have other witnesses that will also testify concerning the work environment in Judge Nelson's office," Lance said.

"Very well, the objection is overruled. Carry on."

Lance thanked the judge and then turned back to Joy. "You may answer the question."

Joy answered the question. Nothing out of the ordinary went on in her father's office during the time she clerked there. When prompted she also admitted that the reason she decided to become a lawyer was because at one time in her life, she hadn't known a more honorable man that Nelson Marshall and she desired to follow in his footsteps.

Joy didn't know if her testimony was helping or hurting her father, but saying nice things about Nelson Marshall felt *mmm good* to her soul.

True to his word, Lance called on numerous current and ex-employees who all verified that Nelson ran a good and honest office. Lance also introduced the theory that Jasmine had been the one who tried to profit from the cases that came through Nelson's courtroom.

When she took the stand, Jasmine tried to be as aloof as possible, but when Lance said, "It burned you up that Nelson's ex-wife was taking half of his money, didn't it?"

Jasmine couldn't hold her tongue any longer. She shot angry darts at Lance as she said, "How would you feel? One day you're living in a half-million dollar house and able to shop and purchase anything you want. Then the next day you're told that the ex-wife is entitled to retain her standard of living, so somebody's standard of living is about to go down. And guess whose that was?" Jasmine angrily pointed at her chest. "My standard of living what cut in half all because," she pointed at Nelson, "his wife was being so greedy. I had to move into a condo and be put on a strict allowance, like I was a child or something." She swung her long curly weave around and then just sat there, waiting for the next question.

Joy couldn't believe that Jasmine was that clueless. That she had no understanding or even care for the family that Nelson left behind. But her arrogance helped the jury to see her motive for going behind Nelson's back and arranging those bribes. Jasmine didn't admit to any wrong doing while on the stand, but no one was deceived.

On the last day of the case, Dontae and Carmella came to court to be with Nelson and Joy when the verdict was read. Dontae was walking with the aid of a cane. His knee was getting better, but it hadn't totally healed as of yet.

Carmella hugged and kissed her daughter. "Ramsey sends his love."

Joy would always be grateful to Ramsey for coming into their lives just when they needed him most. He'd been a father to her and Dontae when their own father had deserted them. As far as Joy was concerned, she now had two fathers.

The court came to order as the jury filed back in. Joy noticed that the members of the jury weren't trying to make eye contact with her father, which was always a bad sign.

The judge turned to the jury and asked, "Has the jury reached a decision?"

"We have, Your Honor," the head juror said.

The decision was handed to the judge; Nelson and Lance stood. Nelson had been charged with five counts of bribery and one count of accessory to commit bribery. The judge informed them that Nelson had been cleared on all five counts of bribery, then everyone held their breath as the judge read the verdict on the last count. "On the count of accessory to commit, the jury finds the defendant... guilty."

Carmella put an arm around both her children and squeezed them tightly. "He'll survive this, so you all need to be strong for your daddy."

"What just happened, Mama?" Joy was shaking her head. She could hardly believe that her father had eluded the bribery charges, but then had been snared by a conspiracy charge. She concluded that, in the final analysis, the jury just couldn't believe that Nelson could live with a woman like Jasmine and not have a clue as to what she had been up to. The time he would get for the accessory charge would be minimal, but Nelson would more than likely lose his license to practice law and that would be devastating. But her mother believed that he would get through it, so Joy would keep the faith as well.

Carmella stayed in her seat as Dontae and Joy went up to the front to hug their father before he was taken away by the guards. It was a sad sight to see, but Nelson Marshall's downfall had been put in motion the day he left his praying wife for someone as selfish as Jasmine Walker.

They hadn't received the total acquittal they had hoped for, but as they left the courtroom the Marshall family, nonetheless, lifted their voices and praised God for His mercy. Because they knew that things could have turned out a lot worse.

Lance approached just as they were leaving the building. He put his hand on Joy's arm and asked, "Can I speak to you for a second?"

"We'll see you back at the house," Carmella told her daughter as she and Dontae walked away.

Lance put his hand in Joy's and began walking with her toward the garage. "I'm sorry that we didn't get a full acquittal, but I promise you that I won't let this go until we can get him acquitted on this accessory count as well."

"You did your best, Lance. I wouldn't have been able to do anything more for him than what you did."

"You know what this means, don't you?" Lance asked with a big grin splattered across his face.

Those dimples of his drove her crazy. She wanted to run her hand down his beautiful face, just so she could touch one of those dimples. "What are you talking about?"

They made it to her car and then he said, "I'm talking about the fact that we don't have any more conflicts of interest between us. So, I'd like to pick you up tonight and take you out to dinner."

"It's about time," Joy just about screamed. "I was beginning to wonder if you were slow or something. I've wanted to go out with you for months." She pulled his head down toward her and kissed him like she'd been loving him for all of her life and had just found a way to show him.

"Whew," Lance said when they broke apart. "If I had known you'd act like this just because of a dinner date, I would have asked you out a lot sooner."

Shoving his shoulder, she said, "Shut up, slow boy. Just make sure you pick me up on time." Joy got in her car and drove off. Life hadn't turned out the way she had expected, but she was amazed at how God was able to break through the cloud of darkness in her life and enable her to enter into a wonderful new day. God was good and she would praise Him for a lifetime.

Dear Reader:

The sermon preached in chapter nine was truly delivered by Pastor Fred Lott of Turning Points Ministry in Charlotte, North Carolina. So if you're ever in Charlotte and looking for a church to attend, you might want to stop in at Turning Points: http://www.turningpointsministries.org/

Join my mailing list:
http://vanessamiller.com/events/join-mailing-list/

Books in the Praise Him Anyhow series
Tears Fall at Night (Book 1 - Praise Him Anyhow Series)
Joy Comes in the Morning (Book 2 - Praise Him Anyhow Series)
A Forever Kind of Love (Book 3 - Praise Him Anyhow Series)
Ramsey's Praise (Book 4 - Praise Him Anyhow Series)
Escape to Love (Book 5 - Praise Him Anyhow Series)
Praise For Christmas (Book 6 - Praise Him Anyhow Series)

His Love Walk (Book 7 - Praise Him Anyhow Series)

Praise Him Anyhow Journal

A Forever Kind of Love

Excerpt of Book 3 in the
Praise Him Anyhow Series

by

Vanessa Miller

Prologue

Looking like a GQ model in his black Armani suit and his yellow tie with tiny black dots, with dimples on both sides of his handsome face, Dontae Marshall put the two-carat Princess cut diamond ring in his pocket. Dontae would have gladly purchased a five-carat ring if need be, but the woman he had fallen in love with didn't hunger and thirst for displays of wealth as the first woman he'd fallen for had.

Dontae was so thankful that his sister, Joy had admonished him to pray about his decision to marry Tory Michaels. He hadn't appreciated the way Joy butted into his business at the time. But after he took that hit on the football field and then had to deal with rehabilitation for his knee, while worrying over his doctor's recommendation that he give up his football career, Dontae discovered that Tory was not the woman for him. She hadn't been in it for the right reasons.

Tory didn't love Dontae Marshall the man; she loved Dontae Marshall the football star. And the day he decided to follow doctor's orders and hang up his helmet, was the day that Tory started bringing him all kinds of drama. In the end, Dontae cut his losses by letting Tory keep that big rock he'd given her and then they both decided to go their separate ways. Soon after Dontae put his full concentration towards building the new career he had mapped out for himself.

It had taken a few years, but Dontae had used the money he'd received as a signing bonus to open a sports agency. Even though he couldn't play the game anymore, he still loved sports, so he sat down and had a talk with Stan Smith, his agent. Stan offered to take Dontae under his wing and he taught him the sports agency business and just like that, Dontae found a new purpose in life. He was passionate about protecting young athletes from some of the nonsense that went on behind the scenes. Dontae believed that his job was to help navigate his clients around a system designed to favor the owners—and sometimes even coaches—rather than the players.

After learning as much as he could from his mentor, Dontae relocated to Charlotte, North Carolina and set up shop. It didn't take long for his agency to gain a good name among the athletic community and his business grew right before his eyes. Dontae's mom had told him that his success was due to the fact that God had been watching out for him. Whether it was God's doing or something much simpler, Dontae didn't care, all he knew was that life was good.

Dontae hadn't imagined that things could get any better, but when he met Jewel Dawson, he realized that God had been holding out on him. Jewel was everything he wanted in a woman. She was soft spoken, yet in command at all times. Jewel was a writer who had taken her career into her own hands and was making a pretty good living. She was daring, loving, beautiful and most of all, she made him smile... no, not just smile, with Jewel, Dontae had learned to laugh and enjoy life again. He picked up the manila envelope, grabbed his keys and headed out the door.

***

Dontae took Jewel to Villa Antonio, her favorite Italian restaurant. The ambiance was perfect for a romantic dinner. Jewel was wearing a sleeveless silk dress that crisscrossed in the back. The dropped waistline on the dress gave way to a skirt designed for twirling movements. Dontae definitely approved. As a matter of fact, he couldn't take his eyes off of her.

"I love this place. I'm so glad you got us reservations here tonight," Jewel said as they were seated in a dimly lit corner of the restaurant.

"I know you love it, that's why we're here."

Jewel leaned over and kissed Dontae on his full, luscious lips. "Thanks baby, you're always thinking about me."

The couple ordered their food and then spent the evening gazing into each other's eyes. Dontae knew with everything in him that Jewel was the one for him. He was ready to make a life with her and didn't want to wait a moment longer. However, getting down on bended knee wasn't an option for him. Oh, he had recovered quite well from his knee injury several years back, but the knee would act up on him at times. And since this was an important moment—one that he wanted Jewel to remember for a lifetime—he didn't want to spoil it by needing the maître d's help when and if he failed to get up on his own.

Jewel's hands were resting on the table. Dontae laid his hands on top of hers, still gazing into his beloved's eyes he said, "Jewel, I want you to know that I am happy when I'm with you. You have brought so much joy into my life and, and—"

"Aw, that's so sweet," Jewel interrupted.

That's when Dontae remembered the ring that was in his jacket pocket. His hand shook with nervousness as he pulled it out and gripped it like he used to hold the football when charging his way to a touchdown. "I just believe that you and I are a perfect match. We fit together, ya' feel me?"

Jewel nodded. "I feel the same way, Dontae. I think I started falling in love with you the moment we met."

That revelation brought a smile to his face, gave him the strength to do what he had gone there to do. He was seated across from Jewel, but suddenly felt miles away. Dontae got up and squeezed in next to his woman. He set the ring box on the table and opened it.

Jewel gasped.

"What I'm trying to say is..."

Jewel wrapped her arms around Dontae and screamed, "Oh my God. Yes, yes, Dontae, I will marry you."

In a joking mood after receiving such a wonderful response to his almost proposal, he waited until she held out her hand for him to put the ring on her finger and then said, "You didn't let me finish my question. How do you know I was going to ask you to marry me? Maybe I just wanted to give you a ring to celebrate our one-year anniversary."

A hint of sadness dimmed Jewel's normally bright eyes. She quickly covered her face and said, "I'm so embarrassed. I should have let you finish. I'm sorry, Dontae."

He couldn't carry the joke any further. The look on Jewel's face told him that he'd gone too far. "No, I'm the one who is sorry. Of course I want to marry you. I was just joking, but I didn't mean to upset you."

Jewel shoved him. "Boy, you play too much."

"I'm sorry about that. But you already agreed to marry me, so you're stuck with me." He took the ring out of the box. "Can I put this on your finger and make it official?"

Grinning from ear to ear, Jewel held out her hand.

Dontae put the ring on her finger; they then celebrated with several kisses and Tiramisu. When they finished off their dessert, Dontae kissed his soon-to-be bride and then grabbed the manila envelope he'd left on the other side of the table and handed it to Jewel. "I almost forgot to give you this."

"What's this?" Jewel asked, while opening the envelope, still grinning at her man.

"Just a little document that I need you to sign and return to my attorney." He leaned back in his seat and added, "At your leisure, of course."

Jewel pulled the document out and read, then stared at it as if the words were written in Greek. After a long silent pause, she turned to him and asked, "Is this a joke?"

Dontae swiveled his head in order to take a glance at the paperwork in Jewel's hand. "No joke, babe, I just need you to sign those papers and return them to my attorney."

"Are you serious?"

"What's wrong?" Dontae asked, not understanding Jewel's reaction.

While shaking her head, Jewel told him, "This is turning out to be the worst proposal in the history of marriage proposals."

Confused by her reaction, Dontae said, "I thought I did good. I brought you to your favorite restaurant. I picked out a diamond that I knew you would love and then I... I—"

"And then you had the audacity to hand me a prenuptial agreement." Jewel threw the document down on the table and yanked the ring off her finger. "If you're so worried that the marriage won't last, I don't think we should even bother getting married in the first place."

Dontae had been leaning back, relaxing and enjoying the moment. But as he watched Jewel take the ring he'd just given her off her finger, a feeling of panic overtook him and he bolted into action. Holding up his hands trying to halt her tirade, Dontae said, "Hold up... you don't need to take that ring off. We're engaged now. I want to marry you."

Jewel put the ring in Dontae's hand and stood up. "Take me home."

"But baby."

"Take me home this instant, Dontae. I don't even want to talk to you right now."

"Baby, be reasonable. Don't you want to discuss the wedding?"

Jewel picked up the prenup, threw it in Dontae's face and then shoved his shoulders until he got up so that she could make her way out of the restaurant.

Dontae could see that he had lost the battle, so he did as Jewel asked so that he would have a shot at winning the war.

1

Carmella Marshall-Thomas was in the kitchen putting the finishing touches on the desserts she had made for Ramsey Jr's coming home party. Her husband's oldest son wasn't moving back to Raleigh as she and Ramsey had hoped, but he would be in Charlotte with Dontae and that was good enough for her. Carmella enjoyed throwing dinner parties for her family, so the Marshalls and Thomases were all gathering together again today.

Raven and Joy were in the kitchen helping her with the meal, while Renee hung out in the family room with Ramsey and Ronny. Dontae was driving in from Charlotte and had promised to pick up Ramsey Jr. from the airport on his way to the house. So as usual everyone would be there except for Ramsey's youngest son, the one with the heart of gold. Rashan was a missionary and had travelled all over the world during his short twenty-eight years of life, helping out and doing the Lord's work wherever needed.

"Okay ladies," Carmella addressed Joy, her natural born daughter and Raven her daughter from her marriage to Ramsey. Carmella and Ramsey had been married for eight years now, and Ramsey's children, the kids with the *R* names, didn't seem like step-children to her anymore. They were family and that's all Carmella had to say about that. "Looks like we have taken care of everything in here. Now all we have to do is set the table."

"Why don't we make Renee do that, since she didn't bother to help us fix one thing today," Raven demanded.

"I second that," Joy said. "Renee acts like she's allergic to pots and pans."

"You two need to leave your sister alone. She contributes to this family in other ways. But one day she will come to understand and appreciate the value of spending time with us in the kitchen," Carmella told her girls even as she prayed for that wish to come true. She so longed to be as close to Renee as she was with the rest of the children. But Carmella had learned the art of patience, so she was willing to wait until Renee felt comfortable enough to have a mother-daughter relationship with her.

"You're just too nice, Mom, that's all that is," Joy told Carmella as she reached into the cabinet and pulled out the fancy china that Carmella only used for family events.

"Why do you always use your best china for us, but use the regular plates for other guests?" Raven asked.

Carmella smiled. She hadn't known that her family noticed her preferences until Joy pulled the right plates out of the cabinet and then Raven commented about it. "You all are the most important people in my life; I wouldn't dare offer anything but the best to my family."

She grabbed hold of Raven's arm, looked her in the eyes and said, "And don't you dare accept anything but the best from the man you choose to marry. You let him know that you're treated like royalty at home and the only way he can get your heart is if he can do better than what your father and I already do."

"You didn't tell me to say any of that to the men I dated," Joy complained.

"Girl, you didn't date all that much and you know it. But by the time you met Lance, I knew he was the one and I knew he would treat you like a queen. So, I didn't need to give you anything to say. I just kept praying that you would wake up and see what was right in front of you." And besides, Carmella had other reasons for saying what she had to Raven. The girl was beautiful, talented and smart, but she had an insecurity about her that caused Carmella to worry that she might let any old riffraff in her life. She didn't want Raven mentally or physically abused by any man, so she kept praying for her daughter.

Smiling as she gazed at the band on her finger, Joy said, "You were right about Lance. That man is so good for me and to me. I'm just glad that I finally gave him a chance."

"Me too," Raven said joyfully, "Your wedding was one of the best I've ever attended, and certainly the best that I ever served as maid of honor for... wait. Did I mention that?"

"Yes, you did," Joy said as she tried to hold in a giggle.

"Forget I said that. I'm throwing all my bridesmaid dressing away. I hereby declare that I will never be another bridesmaid." Raven held her hand up as if she was testifying before congress.

"Here, here," Joy seconded.

Carmella said, "I've already spoken to the good Lord on your behalf; so, believe me when I tell you, Raven, your time is coming." Carmella then picked up the platter holding the roast she had made; roast was Ramsey Jr.'s favorite. "Now, will you ladies help me set the table?"

***

"Man, am I glad to see you. That flight had me calling on the name of Jesus and confessing all my sins," Ramsey Jr. said as he got into Dontae's Range Rover.

"Boy, quit lying. That was only an hour flight, hardly enough time for you to confess *all* the stuff you've done... Don't forget, I know you."

"Shut up and get me away from this airport."

Dontae pulled away from the curb and began driving out of the airport lot. "Flight was that bad, huh?"

"I'm telling you, Dontae, if your Mama wasn't the praying woman that she is, I'd probably be gone on to glory right now."

"Her prayers don't always work; you do know that, don't you." Dontae spoke like a man who'd had first-hand experience in the prayers-not-getting-answered department.

"Real talk... your moms has helped me get through some things these last few years. All of her prayers seem to be working for me." Ramsey Jr. spread out his arms and looked around at the tree lined scenery as Dontae continued driving. "I'm back in North Carolina, aren't I?"

"Where the pollen is high and the women want more than a brother can give."

"I feel a sneeze coming on now. But that's all right. It's only unbearable for about the first couple weeks of spring."

"At least flowers are blooming all over the place in Charlotte," Dontae commented.

"I can hardly wait to get there."

Dontae came to a red light. He stopped the car and turned to his step-brother. "I was thinking..." He hesitated, and then charged on in, "that since you'll be staying with me for a while, I want to introduce you to one of Jewel's sisters. We can double date or something."

Ramsey adamantly shook his head. "Not interested, bro. I just shook off a woman who I didn't know was bipolar until she came at me with a knife. I'm still trying to get my head together from that."

"Come on, Ramsey, I need your help."

With furrowed brows, Ramsey asked, "What are you talking about? Since when do you need help with Jewel? The two of you have been into each other from the moment you met."

Dontae wished he didn't have to talk about what happened between him and Jewel, but he was desperate to get her back and needed help from his brother to make it happen. "We broke up."

"What do you mean, you broke up? You just bought her an engagement ring two weeks ago."

"She gave it back. Got upset when I handed her the prenup."

"I told you it was a bad idea."

"Look, I love Jewel and all, but I'm not about to give her half my money if she decides to leave me for some other man twenty years from now."

"You are such a cynic," Ramsey said, laughing at Dontae's comment.

"No. I'm a realist. And Jewel needs to understand just how real things could get if she or I ever decide to divorce."

"Wow. You and Jewel haven't even gotten married yet, and you're already thinking about divorce."

"Hey, I'm just being a realistic."

"No," Ramsey said, "You're just being cynical and trying to make Jewel pay for something that happened before she met you."

Dontae knew that Ramsey spoke the truth. His father had caused him to be a bit jaded. But dealing with a woman like Tory had also caused Dontae to doubt the reality of happily-ever-after. Once things weren't going the way she wanted them to go, he wasn't hearing sweet nothings from her anymore... seemed like the love Tory had for him just got up and left. If Jewel ever flipped a switch and started acting like Tory, he'd be heartbroken, but he'd still have his money to keep him company, which was why Jewel signing that prenuptial agreement was so important to him.

"Not to bring it up like this, but you are going to be staying at my house rent free. So, I think that one good turn deserves another."

"I'll pay rent if it's that big of a deal. I'm only going to be crashing with you long enough to find my own place anyway," Ramsey reminded Dontae.

Feeling guilty for the unnecessary comment, Dontae back tracked. "I'm not trying to charge you rent. I shouldn't have said it like that. I'm just desperate, man. Jewel is the one for me, so I really need your help."

"Just drop the whole prenup idea and your problem is solved."

Dontae shook his head. The look on his face was set, as if he was thinking about Michael Jordan, Kobe Bryant and all the other brothers who gambled and lost without a prenup. Oh sure, Kobe's wife stayed, but if she had pulled the trigger on that multi-million dollar divorce, Kobe would have been out hocking shirts, shoes and sodas to keep up with his standard of living. "I can't do that. Call me a fool. Call me jaded or whatever. But I just don't believe that people should go into marriage with their heart hanging out of their chest, without stopping to think about what could and probably would end up going wrong down the line."

"If I don't know nothing else, I know about things going horribly wrong," Ramsey said as he leaned back in his seat.

Dontae and Ramsey were both sinfully handsome and successful young men. But they had both experienced trauma that had changed their view of love, faith and

God's ability to handle the things that concerned them. As smart as they were, neither man knew how to get out of his own way.

Ramsey popped up. "Ronny's traveling back to Charlotte with us. He's going to help me get my stuff set up in your house and in a storage unit."

"I can help you with that," Dontae said.

"Not with that knee of yours, you can't. I'm not going to be the one responsible for getting Carmella's boy all banged up again."

"What I mean is, we can pay a service to handle that for you."

"Naw, that's okay. Ronny just lost another job and I'd like to be able to put some money in his hands. And I'd like to spend some time with him before I start my new job. I told dad that I'd figure out what Ronny's next move should be."

Pulling into his mother's driveway, Dontae turned off the car and then asked Ramsey, "Do you think Ronny will help me out?"

Ramsey laughed. "Two women are involved, right?"

Dontae smiled at that. Ronny was definitely a ladies' man. "I forgot who we were talking about." Dontae nodded toward the front door. "You go on in, the family's waiting on you. I'm going to give Jewel's sister a call and tell her it's a go."

Ramsey put his hand on Dontae's shoulder. He had a sincere look on his face as he said, "I know we've only been brothers for the last eight years, but I just want you to know that I'm glad that we are family."

"Yeah, me too," Dontae said as he pulled his cell phone out and made a call to the woman he hoped would be his future sister-in-law.

The first person Dontae saw as he stepped into the house was Lance, his sister's husband. They shook hands and then Lance told him, "Man, am I glad you and Ramsey are here. I'm hungrier than a hostage and Carmella said we couldn't eat until you two rock heads got here."

"Stop." Dontae put up a hand. "I don't think I can handle all the love you're throwing my way."

"Don't get it twisted," Lance told him, "Family is good, but when you're hungry and your mother-in-law cooks like an Iron Chef, food is better."

The two men laughed as they joined the rest of the family. Carmella was busily uncovering the food as Dontae walked into the dining room. She turned and caught a glimpse of her son and then got the biggest grin on her face. "Come on in here, boy. I been waiting all day to give you a hug."

Even though his heart was heavy because of the situation with Jewel, Dontae yet and still smiled back at his mother. He could only remember one time in his life when his mother hadn't been there for him. With the horror stories he'd heard from other men about the things their mothers had done to them, Dontae wasn't about to dwell on one incident. "Hey Moms, I'm happy to see you, too," he said as they hugged. As he peeked over her shoulder, he added, "but I'm even happier to see that mac and cheese on the table."

"See Mom, I told you that I should be your favorite. This boy would take food over you," Joy said as she walked over and hugged her brother.

"Stop all that foolish talk, Joy Lynn. I have been blessed with seven children, two by birth and five by marriage and I love you all with a mother's heart," Carmella declared for everyone's hearing.

After that the family sat down to dinner. They talked, laughed and then played Trivia and Sequence. The ones who weren't playing either game got comfortable on the sofa and watched a movie. If anyone had looked into the Marshall household ten years ago, they never would have believed that all that sadness and dysfunction would one day turn into great joy.

As Ronny, Ramsey and Dontae stood, preparing to take that two hour drive from Raleigh to Charlotte, Carmella remembered something that she needed to tell Dontae. Ramsey and Ronny walked out to the car and Carmella grabbed hold of Dontae's arm and pulled him to the side. "Guess who I saw yesterday?"

Dontae gave her a blank stare. "I wouldn't know where to begin."

"Okay, okay... Coach Linden moved back to town. The school has hired him back and they are throwing an awards banquet for him." The excitement shone through with every word Carmella spoke.

Dontae didn't say anything.

Bringing her excitement down a notch or two, Carmella said, "I thought you'd want to know. I asked him to send the invitations to the banquet to my house because I thought you would want to attend."

A storm was brewing in Dontae's eyes as he said, "I don't want to attend. And I don't want you to go either." He turned and walked out of the house without further explanation.

Ramsey's Praise

Excerpt of Book 4 in the
Praise Him Anyhow Series

by

Vanessa Miller

1

She was standing about six feet away from him, holding a beautiful bridal bouquet when Ramsey Thomas first took notice of her. Long flowing hair, olive skin tone, sparkling hazel colored eyes. The gown she was wearing showed off every bit of her shapely body. Ramsey almost to the point of drooling when his brother Ronny nudged his shoulder and said, "Please tell me you're not drooling over the bride like that?"

Ramsey turned to his brother with furrowed eyebrows. The bride was Jewel Dawson and she was marrying his younger brother, Dontae Marshall. Ramsey was the best man so it would be a bit awkward if he was standing before God and a whole congregation of folks lusting after the bride. "Shut up, idiot. I'm not drooling over Jewel," Ramsey whispered and then turned back around so he could continue taking in the lovely view of Maxine Dawson, Jewel's oldest sister and Maid of Honor.

A few months back Dontae had tried to hook him up with one of the Dawson sisters, but he'd been completely wrong about which one Ramsey would be interested in. Dawn, the middle sister, all though just as beautiful as her other sisters, she was too short for him, and their personalities lending more to them becoming the best of friends rather than having any kind of love connection. But Maxine Dawson was a woman that Ramsey would like to invest some time getting to know.

As if feeling his gaze on her, Maxine's eyes met Ramsey's just as the preacher said, "I now pronounce you man and wife." As Dontae took Jewel in his arms, Ramsey winked at Maxine. He grinned as her cheeks turned red from blushing.

Ramsey wanted to ask her on a date right then and there. But no matter how much Maxine was taking up space in his head, he wouldn't do anything to spoil this moment for his brother.

Later that evening, while at the reception Ramsey was standing with his father, Ramsey senior and his step mother, Carmella when they started in on him. "I guess we'll be attending you wedding next, ay, son?"

Ramsey ignored his father and let his eyes span the room. He was looking for Maxine but he'd never admit that to his father, and certainly not to Mama Carmella. If she knew he had his eye on a woman, she'd start praying and call down Elijah, Mosses and a couple heavenly angels to get Ram to make a move. Ram was the nickname Mama Carmella had given him. His family had taken to calling him that as a way of distinguishing from him and his father.

"Who's that Renee is talking to?" Carmella asked, pointing over by the DJ booth.

Ramsey's head swivel back around. He had three sisters, Joy, Raven and Renee. And he was very protective over all of them. But he tended to watch out for Renee just a bit more. The girl made a career out of finding bad in a room full of good. Ramsey recognized the smooth talker Renee was grinning up at immediately. Marlin Jones was a high powered real-estate developer whom Ramsey had dealt with on occasion. He didn't like the way the man did business. There was something too slick about him. "I'll be back," Ramsey told his parents.

Carmella caught his arm. "Now Ram, don't you go over there bothering your sister. She is old enough to make her own decisions."

"I'm not going to do anything. I know the guy so I just want to say hello." And goodbye, he added under his breath. As Ram pressed forward, Marlin put his hand on Renee's shoulder, her head fell back as she laughed ridiculously at something the man must have said. Marlin must have been telling Renee the funny one about how his tax returns were complete fiction and how the IRS was about to audit him for all of his shenanigans.

"I like the way you laugh. I normally don't come to weddings, but I'm so glad I accepted this invitation," Marlin was saying as Ram advance on them.

"And why is that," Renee asked, beaming up at Marlin.

"Because I met the most beautiful girl in the whole state of North Carolina."

Ram wanted to throw up all over Marlin's playa rap. He only prayed that Renee could see through the him.

But just in case she couldn't he was about to do some playa hating. Ram tapped Marlin on the shoulder and said, "Marlin, I didn't know you were attending my brother's wedding."

Swinging around, Marlin had to lift his head to address Ramsey who was at least a half foot talker than he. "Hey Ramsey, I had no idea that Dontae was your brother. But my mom is best friend's with Jewel's mom so I had to come."

"Gotcha." Ramsey threw a look at Renee and then told Marlin, "Well it was nice seeing you. Do you mind if I have a word with my little sister."

"I thought Charlotte was a big city. But look how small it's suddenly become. I can not believe that this beautiful woman standing next to me is related to someone with a mug like yours," Marlin said lightheartedly.

"Believe it." Ram didn't know how much longer he could hold his fake smile in place, so he quickly put his arm around Renee and began walking away from Marlin. "See you later," Ram said while still smiling and waving.

"What are you up to, Ram?"

"I'm just trying to get you away from that guy."

With a quizzical expression on her face, Renee wanted to know, "Why in the world would you do something like that." She pointed toward Marlin. "The guy is a dream... successful, handsome. There's no bum stamp on his forehead."

"Yeah, but there ought to be a dog stamp on it," Ram replied back.

Rolling her eyes, Renee shoved her brother. "Don't start this stuff tonight, Ram. Just go back to the head table with the rest of the bride and broom party and stay out of my business."

Ram opened his mouth to protest, but Renee lifted her index finger and pointed toward his table. "Go Ram. I'm not going to let you ruin my fun tonight."

He tried to help her. But if his sister wanted to be foolish and fall all over herself for a man who might be in prison in the next year or so, then she could have all the temporary fun she wanted. Ram turned toward the head table and saw Maxine seated next to his chair, eating a piece of wedding cake. So, he took his sister's advice and set about minding his own business. He grabbed a piece of cake off the cake table and then took his seat. "Is this cake as good as you are making it look?"

Maxine picked up her napkin and wiped her mouth. "Did I look like I was starving?"

"You was getting it in that's for sure."

"I deprived myself of all sweets for over a decade. Now that I don't have to worry about being rail thin anymore, I was probably a little too excited about eating this cake."

Ramsey picked up his napkin and wiped the white icing she'd missed from her chin. "Don't worry about it, cake looks good on you."

"I bet you say that to all the girls," Maxine joked as she took another bite of her cake.

Ramsey thought about the line he'd just heard Marlin running on his sister and he didn't want to come across like that. But if he was honest with himself, from the moment he saw her today, he'd been mesmerized. He wanted to get to know this woman in the worst way and he wasn't trying to blow his opportunity by acting like a jerk. "No, I'm not trying to hand you a line. The plain truth is, I think you're beautiful and I would love to take you out some time."

Dontae the groom and Ronny, the all around clown were standing behind. Ramsey hadn't seen them until it was too late. After he told Maxine that he wanted to take her out, both Dontae and Ronny put their hand around their ear and said, "Say what?"

Okay, yeah, when Ramsey first came to the city and Dontae tried to hook him up with one of the Dawson sister, he'd been adamantly against it. He hadn't wanted to be fixed up and Ramsey had just gotten out of an awful relationship with a bipolar woman who made Glenn Close seem like a reasonable woman. So, he needed that hiatus. He turned to his brother and said, "I'm gon' tell y'all like Renee just told me, get somewhere and mind your own business."

Ronny held up a hand. "We know when we're not wanted. And besides we have better things to do than to watch you get shot down."

As he brothers walked off, Ramsey turned back to Maxine. "Excuse them. They weren't raised right." A giggle escaped Maxine's beautiful lips. Ramsey took that opportunity to say, "See, I'm already making you laugh. Imagine how much fun the two of us would have on a date."

"I'm sure it would be wonderful." Maxine couldn't stop grinning. "It's just too bad that you didn't ask me out before I decided to become a mom."

Ramsey's furrowed brows indicated that he didn't get it at all. "I would have never guessed that you were pregnant. When are you due?"

"I'm not pregnant," she said matter-of-factly.

Ramsey took a bite of his cake, took a moment to chew it and then said, "Correct me if I'm wrong, but don't you need to be pregnant in order to become a mom?"

"I would also love to have a husband before I become pregnant." Maxine shrugged. "But since my husband hasn't found me yet, I decided to adopt."

"A little impatient aren't you?"

A ting of regret crossed Maxine's eyes as she said, "The truth is, I thought that I wanted nothing more than to be a model and once my modeling career was over, I'd intended to parley my success into an acting career." She shrugged again, "but I can't act, I'm tired of modeling and since my biological clock is ticking like a time boom, I decided to adopt."

Ramsey was a bit surprised that Maxine had shared so much with him. But maybe she thought of him more like a brother, since her sister had just married his brother. He hoped to God that she didn't think of him that way. Because he sure wasn't seeing a relative when he looked at her. "You look so young. I'm sure you have plenty of time to wait for the right man to come along."

"Like they say, black don't crack," Maxine told him with a smile. "But seriously, I'll be thirty-four this year, so I don't have very many baby making years left."

Ramsey shook his head to that news.

"What?" Maxine asked.

"It's nothing. I'm just amazed that a woman as beautiful as you, hasn't found a man willing to make a baby with you."

"It's more difficult than you think. Most of the men I date are either insecure about my success or they think I'm too controlling."

"I don't know what kind of men you've been dating, but I love me some successful black women."

"Well then, it's too bad for me that you didn't find me before I decided to settle down and become a mother." With that said, Maxine got up and walked away from Ramsey.

Ronny walked back over to the table, leaned over to his brother and said, "Struck out, huh? Should have asked me or Dontae. We could have told you that those Dawson girls ain't no easy win."

***

Books in the Praise Him Anyhow Series

Tears Fall at Night
Joy Comes in the Morning
A Forever Kind of Love
Ramsey's Praise

Escape to Love
Praise For Christmas
His Love Walk

About the Author

Vanessa Miller is a best-selling author, playwright, and motivational speaker. She started writing as a child, spending countless hours either reading or writing poetry, short stories, stage plays and novels. Vanessa's creative endeavors took on new meaning in1994 when she became a Christian. Since then, her writing has been centered on themes of redemption, often focusing on characters facing multi-dimensional struggles.

Vanessa's novels have received rave reviews, with several appearing on *Essence Magazine's* Bestseller's List. Miller's work has receiving numerous awards, including "Best Christian Fiction Mahogany Award" and the "Red Rose Award for Excellence in Christian Fiction." Miller graduated from Capital University with a degree in Organizational Communication. She is an ordained minister in her church, explaining, "God has called me to minister to readers and to help them rediscover their place with the Lord."

Vanessa has recently completed the For Your Love series for Kimani Romance and How Sweet the Sound for Abingdon Press, first book in a historical set in the Gospel era which releases March 2014. Vanessa is currently working on an ebook series of novellas in the Praise Him Anyhow series. She is also working on the My Soul to Keep series for Whitaker House.

Vanessa Miller's website address is: www.vanessamiller.com But you can also stay in touch with Vanessa by joining her mailing list @ http://vanessamiller.com/events/join-mailing-list/ Vanessa can also be reached at these other sites as well:

Join me on Facebook: https://www.facebook.com/groups/77899021863/
Join me on Twitter: https://www.twitter.com/vanessamiller01
Vie my info on Amazon: https://www.amazon.com/author/vanessamiller